DATE DUE		
8-28	JAN 17 1996	
9-2	NOV 9 1999	
9-13	JAN 18 2000	
9-24	AUG 0 5 2000	
10-8		
10-12	JAN 1 0 2005	
10-22	JUL 01	
11-13	JUL 17 2004	
12-4		
DEC 1 8 1991		
JUL 2 4 1992		

The
PERFECT
MURDER

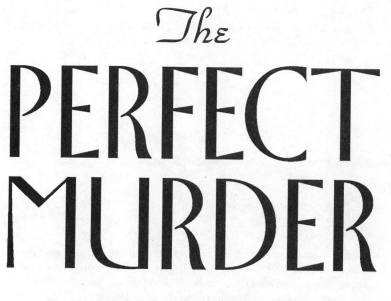

The
PERFECT
MURDER

FIVE GREAT MYSTERY WRITERS
CREATE THE PERFECT CRIME...

Jack Hitt
with
Lawrence Block • Sarah Caudwell
Tony Hillerman • Peter Lovesey
Donald E. Westlake

HarperCollins*Publishers*

FIRST EDITION

Designed by Cassandra J. Pappas

Library of Congress Cataloging-in-Publication Data

The Perfect murder : five great mystery writers create the perfect
  crime / [edited] by Jack Hitt ; with Lawrence Block . . . [et al.].—
  1st ed.
    p.   cm.
  ISBN 0-06-016340-2
  1. Detective and mystery stories, American.   2. Detective and
mystery stories, English.   3. Crime—Fiction.   I. Hitt, Jack.
II. Block, Lawrence.
PS648.D4P48   1991
813′.087208—dc20   90-55965

91 92 93 94 95 NK/HC 10 9 8 7 6 5 4 3 2 1

PREFACE

The perfect murder is a quest as old as man. Cain attempted it first and failed first. His alibi—"Am I my brother's keeper?"—was a legendary attempt to point suspicion in another direction. But because suspects in Eden at the time were few (four, counting the snake), the process of elimination was fairly efficient. Since then, Cain and his intellectual progeny have been prolific. Every generation has seen more than one mad genius bring his or her wit to bear on the technology and circumstances of the day to carry out the perfect murder. And there has always been some detective just as eager to put the same caliber of wit to the task of catching the killer. From this competition came the literary genre known as the murder mystery.

With few exceptions, the murder mystery is always told from the detective's point of view. The narrative of catching the killer is not only the most sensible structure for a good plot, but also the most morally safe. The author gets to peer into the darkest folds of the human psyche from the high moral ground of successful law enforcement. Not long ago,

v

in the pages of *Harper's Magazine*, I set out to shuffle the
players, the plot, and the outcome of this literary tradition.
As a conversational device, I created the character of "Tim,"
a man with a nineties sensibility and eighties wealth. For
reasons of both art and convenience, Tim decides that he
must murder his wife, but doesn't know how to go about it.
So he hires five mystery writers to serve as his consultants.
As a man of the nineties, Tim dares not take a step without
soliciting the opinion of his advisors. Tim believes that if
politicians must do it, then it only makes sense that murderers
should as well. The original *Harper's* article was published as
the minutes of a meeting between Tim and his novel em-
ployees. Afterwards, it struck Tim that as helpful as it might
be to get everyone's opinion over lunch, it would better suit
his ends if he allowed hs consultants to ponder their individual solutions to his problem over time and on paper. Thus,
beginning again, Tim wrote a letter to his five advisors and
began an exchange. What follows is a year's worth of correspondence, all in pursuit of the murder most appropriate
to the time we live in and the people we are.

The
PERFECT
MURDER

FROM TIM

I write you because I have so many complaints about the fine art of murder and how it has been debauched in our time. One can hardly pick up a newspaper without reading of someone being stabbed or shot or shoved in front of a passing train or car. How sad. Like so many fans, I yearn for the old days when the cocktail chatter among society swells flourished with news of methods, motives, designs, and craftsmanship. Think of Robert Walker in Alfred Hitchcock's *Strangers on a Train* when he asked those two beaming grande dames how they might kill their husbands. The conversation came alive! Pros and cons were batted back and forth. And with a candor too uncommon today, the dowagers weighed the competing virtues of the noose and the dirk.

I think murder, like so many of its sister arts, has been destroyed by the hideously leveling force of capitalism. The finest practitioners have sold out, and all the arts have been cheapened. Alas, it is everywhere. Who doesn't wince upon hearing our operatic divas squawk Christmas ballads each

1

year to make a few extra dollars? Who can stand to see our finest thespians on television pimping the newest denture adhesive or hemorrhoid ointment? Our novelists are reduced to doing the work of press agents, and our poets churn out doggerel for third-rate political candidates. Yet, from time to time, some great artist emerges from the common herd to restore some tired genre with a fresh approach, to shake the old forms free of received gimmicks and clichés. Murder, too, is in need of an artist.

As I write you, I have just completed breakfast, all the members of my household have left, and I am alone to contemplate this morning's headline. It reads, MAN SHREDS NEIGHBOR IN WOODCHIPPER. I am not certain I need tell you the details of the killing, because what seizes anyone's imagination in this story seized the headline writer's as well. It's that woodchipper. The rest is tiresomely familiar. Two men, a robbery involving a huge sum—you know the rest.

Perhaps the most subtle sentence in the entire story is this one: "A woodchipper is a common appliance in contemporary American suburbs meant to handle wood items up to 18 inches in length and 10 inches in diameter." Pity the poor hack who wanted so desperately to take flight from the facts and describe the Grand Guignol that is—despite ourselves—taking shape in our minds. Instead he must bait the reader's imagination with a sentence that sounds as if it were taken from the machine's instruction manual. Fortunately, it is enough. Every reader who reads this scene conjures up the proper assortment of images: a saw hastily retrieved from the workbench, a bloody bathtub, and a crude lesson in Gray's anatomy. And maybe we contemplate the whirr of the latest catalog appliance being pressed into macabre service.

Moving on, the reader encounters the obligatory quotation from the local constable. He tells us in the charmingly flat prose of the precinct house that "the evidence consists exclusively of fingernail bits and skin flakes found adhered to the leaves of an oak tree by the river behind the house." You have to love this man. "Adhered," he says! As if the word were a term of art in his line of work. And listen to the lyrical flow of those prepositional phrases. ". . . to the leaves of an oak tree by the river behind the house." This is the poetry of the common man.

The quotation is especially important because a successful crime reporter knows that when he writes he must tell two stories. The first is a crude outline of a narrative, the cold objective facts of the case that construct the bare framework of the story. This is a story restricted in form by the public's allegedly prim taste and a city editor's cowardice. The other story is actually not written by the reporter at all. It is merely alluded to, a silhouette of a story lurking behind the first. But it is the richer of the two, full of detail, action, and meaning. The author of this story is none other than the reader himself, who shades in the outline supplied by the newspaper with his obscene imagination.

In the course of contemplating this phantom story, our eyes are pulled back to one word by the policeman. We consider it again: "exclusively." And we realize that the evidence is very, very slight. A mild qualm troubles the morning's reverie. Somewhere in the back of our mind, one lone synapse—confined to a corner of the subconscious so far away from our surface reading of the story that we are scarcely aware—flicks off a single, lambent thought: if only the killer had wheeled the woodchipper a little closer to the water he wouldn't have been caught.

3

Can it be true? That we wish him to *get away* with this crime? Of course, it's true! Because what really attracts us to this story—whether we are sitting in our housecoats after breakfast, or catching a paragraph or two at a red light on the way to work, or absorbing the details as we roar along in the common carrier—is the novelty of that damned woodchipper. In some strange way, we wish to reward this man, privately, each to ourselves, with our regret over his loss of liberty for taking an act so wretchedly common these days and endowing it with a certain freshness. I believe there is an entire school of thought that considers such cleverness to be the very soul of genius.

Murder needs a great artist, my friends, and I am that man. I am a journeyman now, like so many of your readers. I have perused the great books, your books, which I count as *theoretical* musing on the art. I have read the newspapers and nonfictional accounts—which, like a remainder stall in a bookstore, alert us to the most notorious failures. I am like so many of your readers, only I am bold enough to graduate from my apprenticeship. I wish to take my diploma. Remove my aprons. Join the guild. Do you know what I mean? I am ready to take theory into practice. And like any good student, I turn to my mentors for advice. Let's face it. These are the nineties, the *fin de siècle*, and no great artist in any modern discipline—whether fiction, politics, business, music, or what have you—can dare take that step without the proper coaches, experts, and technicians. In short, like any modern man, I need my consultants.

Certainly you will agree that murder—and I shall call it what it is; what good is euphemism among intimates!—is an art. I have built my theory upon the ground broken by Thomas De Quincey in his excellent essay, "On Murder,

Considered as One of the Fine Arts." (I may be an apprentice, but I have done my homework.) De Quincey coyly addresses what I freely admit to you in this letter: that murder has its charms and attractions when committed with a sense of aesthetics. How much all of us are driven, in De Quincey's words, "to graze the brink of horror."

De Quincey seeks to strip the veneer of etiquette from murder and thereby contemplate its hidden beauty. He does this by considering one of its sister arts, the common house fire: "And in any case, after we have paid our tribute of regret to the affair considered as a calamity, inevitably, and without restraint, we go on to consider it as a stage spectacle. Exclamations of 'How grand!' 'How magnificent!' arise in a sort of rapture from the crowd."

Murder too is greeted with such a rapture. Only, murder being what it is, we must express ourselves in the key of moral revulsion and make our aesthetic judgments in the language of disgust. All murder is denounced as villainous or horrible or ghastly. But it is not difficult to translate these flaccid euphemisms. In these words, the good critic can hear the subtle shadings of the aesthete, grappling with questions of taste both good and bad, and of craft both pedestrian and sublime. Unlike when one reads the vocabulary of literary criticism, one needn't leaf through the pages of an appendix in order to translate the specialty's jargon. In this fine art, our vocabulary shouts at us every day from the front pages. And on those pages, one can find the elements of an art as ancient as Cain himself, our founding father.

Consider the most unoriginal murders, the simple braining with a rock or stabbing with a knife. Our headline writers feebly call such killings: troubling, disturbing, perplexing, harrowing, vexing, galling, or agonizing. But then what murder isn't any of these? Such adjectives combine the severest criticism with the faintest praise. What we mean with such words is that the murder is simply bad, both in motive and in means. It is "troubling" because it is uninteresting in every way, and it is "vexing" because we are at a loss to guess why anyone would risk prison for something so uninspiring. Any schoolmarm would give this work an F.

Then we have the catalog of nouns used to condemn as merely average the murderer who has employed a common method, only to excess. We call the man: brute, savage, ruffian, barbarian, desperado, ghoul, ogre, beast, fiend, cutthroat, villain, miscreant, wretch, reptile, monster, hellhound, cur, dog, mongrel, or animal. This murderer is a distinct amateur who instead of stabbing his victim once, perhaps stabbed his victim fifteen times. Repetition does not art make. Our killer gets a D.

But he is getting better, is he not? So let's move on. One more step up the ladder of praise and he or his crime is condemned as: indifferent, cold, senseless, callous, thoughtless, and pointless. At this level of criticism, the act of killing is still of little interest but we hear in such language a condemnation of the amateur's foolishness. An opening, as it were, had been made. The stage had been set, the curtains had parted, but our protagonist came to the proscenium in a pratfall. I think of a man who recently drove his entire family to an isolated bridge and hurled them off one at a time only to discover later that not only had they all swum to shore safely but that a den of Cub Scouts had witnessed the entire fiasco from a nearby scenic viewpoint. At this level, our man has let us down, and so we describe his killing as "indifferent" not so much because *he* is but because *we* are. It is "senseless" because *we* can make no sense of it, and "thoughtless" because so little thought went into the act. It is "pointless" because it can be neither praised nor derided. Still, a C.

Just above this echelon we find the vast majority of murders. We are now solidly in the realm of aesthetic criticism. We can sense the hand of the artist but we think the execution still lacks a certain polish. I am thinking of the fellow who opened up the possibility of marriage for himself and his lover by locking her husband (a zoologist at the local zoo) in the cage of a panther after everyone else had left work. I admire the effort involved here—the beginnings of a theme, perhaps even an extended conceit, an attempt at unity. Unfortunately, his genius was captured on the videotape of a security camera. Behold the perils of the modern age, ladies and gentlemen.

In murders at this level there is a sense of disappointment but praise for a job well done, however much it may have failed. And there are so many of these killings that we have a great multitude of words: heinous, wicked, infamous, depraved, brutal, atrocious, vicious, unconscionable, unjustifiable, indefensible, inexcusable, unpardonable, irremissible, disgraceful, despicable, scandalous, outrageous, immoral, unwarranted, undeserved, unmerited, scurrilous, perfidious, treacherous, contemptible, cowardly, craven, dastardly, detestable, deplorable. Just reading the list, one can hear the critic's connotation, the frustration of promise undelivered. "Unmerited," we say, suggesting so subtly that it might have been "merited." "Disgraceful," we say, knowing that what we mean is that it might have been "graceful." There is a deep sadness in these killings, but unfortunately the killer must leave with nothing more than a white ribbon and our thanks for participating. A C+.

Now we have arrived to the very threshold of art. Now we are talking about murder worthy of the word. Now we are using the vocabulary of praise, and, obversely, we are calling the murder: ghastly, revolting, unseemly, base, foul, gross, vile, odious, loathful, execrable, abhorrent, fulsome, grisly, gruesome, grotesque, hideous, repulsive, horrid, repugnant, nauseating, sickening, or offensive. These words have heat in them because in the language of murder we must revile most what we like best. Now this is a crime worth committing, worth doing, and, judging from the details released by the police, we think it's pretty good. I situate our man with the woodchipper at this level. The language implies premeditation, and certainly some creativity went into the means. We see some planning, some design, a scheme, and we like it. Our schoolmarm awards a B.

The next echelon lands us squarely in the realm of the artist. Our chroniclers are howling that our auteur is: heartless, pitiless, merciless, or ruthless. Although mass murderers rarely fit into any of the categories I have been discussing (again, volume is not often the source of art), the high honor of this level of achievement could arguably go to the fifteenth-century Baron Gilles de Rais. Not only was he a great patron of Joan of Arc's campaigns and a champion of the theater (he converted many of his castles to public stages), the baron managed to convince others to practice his art for him. Gilles de Rais would actually stage his unique dramas, have them carried out by his servants, and sit back as an audience of *one*. He attended several hundred such productions—some say eight hundred—before the bishop of Nantes could no longer abide his indulgences, even from an aristocrat who underwrote the Crusades, and had him and nearly twenty of his stagehands burned at the stake. This kind of killer is no longer an amateur. He has committed a crime both rare and interesting. One that excites the public's wits. He has slipped the tethers that bind any journeyman: mercy, pity, ruth. He has transcended the mundane and arrived at that critical plane the fifth-century literary critic Longinus recognized as true art: that which *transports* us. Welcome to the world of the imagination.

We grow giddy now, do we not? We are in the high ether of murder, breathing its thin but rare bouquet. We are now talking about gradations of genius, nuanced levels of novelty, visitations by the intoxicating afflatus. The headline writers know this and tell us not in words—because there are no words!—but in phrases suggesting that the mere reading of the account will effect in the reader an altered state. This is murder that chills one's spine, stops one's breath, curdles one's blood, makes one's flesh creep, stands one's hair on end, makes one shudder, chills one's bones, or makes one's blood run cold. This is great art, inspiring ecstasy—literally *ex stasis* or "out of body." Books will be written about this murderer—one must think of Jeffrey MacDonald—as surely as books have been written about Michelangelo or T. S. Eliot.

Finally we come to the vocabulary of highest praise. These are the words reserved for that artist who comes along perhaps only once a generation or a century. And we damn him with the fiercest words possible. I can think of only a few who merit this kind of praise. Jack the Ripper continues to fascinate on so many levels. To reread the accounts of his work is similar to the sensation of returning to the hyperpopulated canvases of Hieronymous Bosch—each visit to the work reveals so many beautiful things we didn't see last time. I also think of Leopold and Loeb, the two young men who sought to use our art to reveal the triumph of pure reason in a time of rampant irrationality. They killed a man for *no reason* whatsoever, only to prove that they could do it. That they didn't get away with it because one of them dropped his eyeglasses doesn't detract from their thinking. The entire concept is thoroughly original. Their motive was nothing at all. Perhaps the scientists are right when they tell us that there is nothing as beautiful as a vacuum. Yet, can we praise these men? These Homers and Mozarts of our art? No, we must rage and invoke the language of Hades: satanic, diabolical, hellish, infernal, fiendish, demoniacal, and (my favorite) Mephistophelean. We curse Satan when we mean to praise God! We stutter, "How diabolical!" when we wish to lick our wanton lips and purr, "How divine!"

Not only is the appraisal of murder cast in the language of euphemism, but the entire affair is appreciated at a safe remove. The mystery novel itself is nothing more than euphemism elevated to genre. The books are not about the murderer, but about the detective catching the murderer. The contemplation of murder is not unlike the viewing of an eclipse, I suppose. We must look upon it indirectly, we must see it through a series of mirrors or refractions. We are all Jasons peering into the face of the Gorgon by way of the looking glass. For the murder mystery, the mirror is the detective himself.

Few people, actually, care about the detective. We care only about the murderer. But conscience still has a queer—albeit, these days, tenuous—grip on the average citizen. Tradition holds that we cannot call ourselves members of the society of proper men and women *and* openly enjoy the genius of a murderer. So we express our appreciation for the cunning of the detective. We admire the gumshoe's street smarts, the tidiness of deductive reasoning, and the easy pathways of the cruciverbalist's mind. These are the means to glimpse the superior concoctions of the killer. But isn't it all an elaborate disguise? To return to the beginning (more or less), who cares for Sherlock Holmes when he sits alone in his study, mainlining cocaine and knocking off monographs on tobacco ashes? It is Professor Moriarty who continually excites our imaginations. He is always the genius, address unknown, lurking in the shadows of London's foggy alleys.

It may seem that what I am pursuing is nothing more than the perfect murder. But consider how mundane even that modest aspiration actually is. The perfect murder, as defined by the amateurs and the dilettantes of crime, is nothing more than a murder after which the killer doesn't get caught. That is too easy. A simple reading of FBI statistics reveals that an overwhelming number of murders go unsolved. Perfect murders are *easy*, in fact easier in some way than the flawed variety. Who cannot plunge a dagger into a stranger's neck and live out a life unmolested? Who cannot poison a close relative—without motive—and remain beyond suspicion? That is a poltroon's game, played every day, and perfunctorily. No, what I seek is not the perfect murder, but the perfect masterpiece. I wish to commit a crime so beautiful in construction and so ingenious in practice that it aspires to the condition of art. I want a murder baroque in concept and rich in detail. When it is all done, I will spend the autumn of my life writing my memoirs and will instruct my estate to publish the book after my own death. This account—laying out both theory and practice—will stand as my contribution to the reintroduction of murder to the muses. My book will explain everything in such detail that scholars will pore over it with the same care they spend ferreting out the recondite allusions of *Ulysses* or parsing the extraordinary syntax of a Marcel Proust or a Henry James.

In the quattrocento, the great Italian masters practiced their art on a modest piece of cloth stretched by four boards. They prayed for the chance to take on the greatest canvas of all—the cathedral. Inside a great duomo, they hoped to tell a great story through the multitude of painterly techniques learned on the smaller fields. They were the cathedral builders, still recognized today for the forethought, artisanship, and genius that went into their opus magnum. I too wish to build a monument more lasting than bronze or stone—a cathedral of such scope and detail that everyone will recognize it as genius and as art.

If you are interested in my idea (and I assume that you are), I must now tell you of myself and of my circumstances. I was a child of common birth who, as politicians love to say, "rose above my circumstances." I am a man of education, an alleged businessman, and I am extremely rich. My wealth, however, comes not from my tedious little company but almost entirely from my wife. But, because of the way things have fallen out, I have access to enormous sums of money. I mention this only to liberate your own thinking. Should your solution to my problem require vast amounts of capital, travel, preparation, or research, I am amply provided for, and can easily arrange it.

I studied to be a doctor once but was able to marry my way out of such a godforsaken profession. I only mention this because you should be aware that any proposal that makes use of medicines and other concoctions will have to deal with the fact that I am not unaware of certain remedies and poisons. Any pharmacological solution will have to deal with the fact that I long prepared to master the craft. But, then, this is America, who isn't comfortable in a drugstore?

My house is a three-story affair. My wife and I sleep in separate bedrooms—hers on the third floor and mine on the second. We have a maid who comes Monday, Wednesday, and Friday. And both of us make use of a chauffeur, whose sympathies tend toward my own.

My wife? Well, the less said the better. To know anyone is to empathize with them, isn't that true? But you must know the basics, I suppose. She is a woman of excessive appetites whether at the table, in bed, in society, or in the stores. She is attractive, middle-aged, and is given to outrageous manipulation. I could go into the details of how she received all her father's money (leaving her two sisters in the cruel position in which I once found myself: forced to marry money rather than make it), but it is a story so familiar that it is the concept behind a thousand books. Her current obsession is the cause of my grief and of my inspiration. She is having an affair with my best friend, and neither suspects that I know.

He—that is, the man who has set upon my head the horns of the cuckold—is no innocent. But then, what man is when it comes to such matters? He simply chose not to think with his head or his heart. He succumbed to the oldest temptation. For our purposes, let us call this man Blazes Boylan. What can I tell you of this poor slob? That he is a businessman, that he is divorced, that he was once my best friend? I am resisting the desire to paint him as a fool. Even though he is, although no more a fool than most of the members of our wretched sex. Blazes was born to all the comforts and privileges life in this country offers a man willing to learn to read. He has made a considerable fortune.

13

But, in America, becoming rich requires only the concentration of one's mind and the suspension of one's morals. Like so many men, Blazes suffers from an unidentified ennui. It is a sense of boredom that has suffused his character so profoundly and so serenely that he thinks having an affair is an act of danger and triumph. As I said, he is an average man.

I saw Blazes at the club the other day. He tried desperately to keep up the appearance of our friendship. He didn't do nearly as good a job as I did. We were sitting in the parlor drinking coffee. I replaced my cup gingerly atop my saucer and grunted, in the way we men are supposed to do, "So, my bachelor friend, getting any these days?" Were this a movie, no doubt the hapless Blazes would knock his cup onto the floor. But this is real life, and, as I said, Blazes is only as foolish as most men. He grunted right back, in the way we men are supposed to do, "Wish I were!" But his eyes—it's always the eyes—tightened ever so gently at the corners, revealing the unexpected horror of this conversation. My eyes lit up sweet and boyish, as if we had just finished chucking each other on the shoulder. My eyes are my most precious asset.

All of this is beginning to sound rather familiar, isn't it? Why shouldn't it? I would not be writing you if I could give this familiar story an extraordinary ending. As it is, this story is tediously ordinary. It is up to you to raise it to the status of Homer with an unordinary finale. As a framework for that ending, I fancy that my wife should be the recipient of your respective talents, that I should wind up free, and that the unthinking Blazes should find himself in the dock incapable of presenting a convincing alibi against the ample evidence so painstakingly discovered by the police detectives.

14

Moreover, this evidence must be so compelling that it completely refutes the police's well-founded, initial suspicion of me. That would be a story worth telling.

There is one other detail you should know. Unlike my wife, Blazes is a fellow of specific and timely habits. Yet in one habit, they are both flawlessly punctual. At 5:00 P.M. every Monday, Wednesday, and Friday, he leaves his office to walk home. At the same hour, my wife leaves to take her afternoon constitutional. They meet at a nearby inn, share a drink in the bar, and leave separately by 5:30 P.M. They both arrive a few minutes later, entering separately again (she first, he second) and meeting in Room 1507. At 6:30 P.M., they both exit separately (he first, she second). By 7:00 P.M., like clockwork, she is back at our house, seated and ready to dine with me.

It is I who, day after day, must look across the supper table at a face one might think is flushed with romance. But in fact it is the glow of another joy, the great pleasure of the practical joke, the bliss of the secret well kept, the happiness of the rug merchant hoodwinking a tourist at the bazaar. She fancies that I sit like a boob at my end of the table, oblivious to the last hour of humiliations. I do nothing to make her think otherwise.

In that regard, we are very much the same person. She bears me no ill will, actually. In some perverse manner (one that only comes with this kind of money), she loves me in the way that I love her. Were I to confront her with her cruelties, she would insist that she meant none of it. And she would be telling the truth. This is but a game to her. I am simply the other player. She wishes to play her game with no one but me. And I her. I only wish to change the game.

Now you ask, can I pull this off? Am I capable of arranging the most complicated, artful murder of the century and carrying it out with dash and élan? Of course. I am a man after my own wife's heart. Moreover, I am a man. What man is not schooled in the labyrinthine complexities of mendacity? What man cannot lie and maintain the mask of wounded candor? We men have such extensive practice. We lie so often in our lives. Every time a man utters the words "I love you," he carries forth one of the most enduring lies of the human situation. That, I submit, is proof enough of my ability. Otherwise, I urge you to reread this letter.

Is the public ready for the cold honesty you and I demand of them? I think so. This is the end of the Age of Freud, an era obsessed with revelation and candor. Throughout our society we continually see those who have laid bare uncomfortable realities to an audience that roars kudos and tosses bouquets of roses. In our time, we have seen yesterday's perverts become today's sex therapists. They confess (and in such wicked detail!) their particular quirks and kinks in bestselling "self-help books." The dominatrix of old probably has her own talk show today and dispenses her techniques like some fly fisherman on public television. Only a few decades ago, we disguised the foulest passions of the human heart with the polite vocabulary promoted by Amy Vanderbilt. Today, all etiquette is dead. We are told it is better to spew our bile *honestly*—to tell, however cruel, the bitter truth to those we love—than to suppress it. Our politicians confess their various maladies—alcoholism, gambling, malfeasance—in the space of a television commercial, and are hailed as statesmen for it. Everyone is coming clean. I saw on the Phil Donahue show the other day that the Satanists have abandoned their dark covens and joined the United Council of Churches. Is the public ready for candor

16

from the likes of me? My friends, they are howling for it.

Murder is ready, then. An old art form is reborn. You and I stand poised at the border; ready, in the words of De Quincey, "to graze the brink of horror." Let us seize the aesthetics of this new art and mold them in our fashion. We shall be the Bloomsbury Group of murder, a founding generation who will shape the postmodern killing. We shall strip the world of its last language of euphemism and set it free to contemplate and enjoy the world's finest art form. You shall be seen as its authors and I shall be your Stephen Dedalus. We shall make Joyce's greatest words come true again: "I go to encounter for the millionth time the reality of experience and to forge in the smithy of my soul the uncreated conscience of my race." And you will be my father and my mother. You, my artificers! Stand me now and ever in good stead!

FROM DONALD E. WESTLAKE

DEAR FRIEND,

I have received your recent letter, and I have thought long and seriously about it, and this is my response. What your story demonstrates initially is that it is never too late to begin acting sensibly. You yourself will, I think, admit that your choices till now have been less than satisfactory. Let us begin by recapping the erroneous steps that have led you to this impasse; an impasse at which, happily, you seem at least to have delved deep within yourself to tap some previously unsuspected lode of wit and make the *right* move for a change, by turning to experts for their guidance and counsel. Would you install your own plumbing? Take out your own adenoids? Prepare your own tax return? Park your own car at a better restaurant? Of course not. In the very nick of time, at the ultimate brink of fate, you have suddenly realized what we all must sooner or later acknowledge: You need help.

What were the unsound measures that led you to your current predicament? I would begin with the fine education you somehow received, though you describe your background as "common" and seem to have had no money till you married. This fact suggests a native intelligence you only sporadically demonstrate in the potted history you have provided. Either you got your education through the winning of a scholarship, or you struck the fancy of some benefactor; both possibilities require the possession of a nimble wit.

But, having attained an education far superior to that which destiny might seem to have intended for you—hark back if you will to the educational histories of your childhood chums—what did you do with the opportunity? Very little. Did you prepare yourself to cut a swath through any of the arts or professions? Not at all. You seem to have been content to use the advantages thrust upon you merely to give yourself a pleasing veneer of culture and civilization. In brief, my friend, you sold yourself short. Given native ability, plus opportunity, you did no more than prepare yourself to be a rich woman's lap dog. And now, constricted by the role you freely chose for yourself, you come whining to *me* to pull you from the mire.

Very well, very well, reproofs are idle at this point. It is not my intention, in fact, to rub your nose in your own inadequacies, since you were intelligent enough to note them for yourself and to ask for aid; though rather late in the day. But it is important that you have a clear view of your own proclivities and impedimenta, if you are to rise above them and succeed at *something* at last.

So. To go on with the descending path of your career, you say you studied at one time to be a doctor, but that you failed to complete those studies, and so today have only a smattering of medical knowledge. This, I take it, would be a part of that education you so fortunately came by, and is further indication that you either squandered the scholarship you'd won or betrayed your benefactor's benevolence. Here is an early suggestion that, though capable of thinking in terms of long-range gains and goals, when put to the test you lack the stamina, initiative, élan, self-confidence, call it what you will, for the long haul. (A not insignificant fact, given the project you now contemplate, and on the behalf of which you have come to me.)

Having proved yourself a dilettante by the time you'd finished the educational process, it is clear that you then made small or no efforts to secure your future through your own talents and accomplishments, but looked about for someone to marry who could support you in the style to which you longed to become accustomed. (It is this fact which tends me to favor the benefactor theory in re your education, as opposed to an earned scholarship. I see, perhaps, an unworldly widow, or a lonely homosexual music teacher of a certain age.)

But even in choosing the path of least resistance, you somehow seem to lack the capacity to follow through. You married a rich woman. Clearly, the bargain, whether stated or tacit, was this: You would be her husband. She would give you access to her wealth. But did you keep the bargain, once it was agreed to? You and your wife not only don't share a bed, or a bedroom, you don't even share a *floor*. She sleeps on the third, you on the second. You will probably claim it was her wish to arrange your private accommodations that way, but even if that's true, how strongly did you try to persuade her out of it? Weren't you secretly pleased at the opportunity thus provided to distance yourself from your wife, from, to be blunt, your shame of *not* living up to your end of the bargain? Surely it is your attitude toward the woman, as well as any defects in her (which would have been known to you prior to the wedding, when they weighed so much less than her bank balance), which led her to Blazes Boylan and the current situation.

So here you are, a patina'd underachiever in chafing bondage to a contemptuous rich wife. Your thoughts, rationally enough, turn to murder. Fortunately for yourself, to judge by your own hesitant plans (as hinted at in your letter), you decided to seek expert counsel before undertaking the project.

Oh? Did you think I wouldn't notice as you hinted at your own solutions to the problem, dropping them in slyly, as though innocently, in the hope (doomed, I'm afraid) of professional praise? Think about it; if I were obtuse, you wouldn't have come to me.

What were those suggestions you offered so coyly? Well, there was the "pharmacological solution," to use your term, by which of course you meant poison. My dear sir, *you studied to be a doctor!* Don't you think the police will investigate your background? They will, I assure you, and do so much more exhaustively, I may say, than you have offered it up to inspection in your letter to me. If the police are presented with a woman dead by poisoning, whose husband had once studied to be a doctor, they will not for a second be duped or distracted, not by all the false trails and false alibis in the world. Your cleverness, plus mine, plus as much more cleverness as you can bring into play from other sources, will all be wasted against the blunt wall of their conviction. And yours; for murder.

Let me emphasize a point I know you know, but believe you perhaps do not really believe. When a married woman is murdered, the police *always* concentrate their attention on the husband. The only exception I know is the case where the actual murderer is found at the scene of the crime in flagrante delicto, and even then, you may be sure the police will not fail to satisfy themselves that the husband didn't instigate the matter.

Police suspicion is to be diverted from the husband only with the greatest difficulty, even in the simplest and cleanest of situations. *Add* the slightest detail to their preexisting suspicion, and it will not be diverted at all. If you were an airline pilot, you should not bomb your wife; if a carpenter, not tap her with a hammer; if a magician, not saw her in half; if an editor, not cut her to pieces. And if you once upon a time studied to be a doctor, leave the poison on the shelf. I hope I make myself clear.

And what is another of your hints, another of your plans in embryo? You are very obviously, my dear chap, toying with the idea of taking into your confidence the chauffeur whose professional services you share with your wife, but whose "sympathies," to quote you, you suspect to tend in your direction.

What? Take an *employee* into your confidence? Place yourself at the very real risk of exposure or blackmail on the basis of the calculated "sympathy" of a fellow whose main thoughts when in converse with you must be of his job security and his Christmas bonus? In his driving of you or your wife on your separate errands, won't the both of you from time to time have engaged him in conversation? And won't he, the sensible servant I presume him to be (because the very rich can afford sensible servants, and quite often absolutely need them), express "sympathetic" reactions to you both? And on the basis of this pecuniary bonhomie you would risk your success, your freedom, and your future? By Harry, sir, you came to me just in time.

Again, in emphasizing the access you hold to "enormous sums of money" (you aren't a drug dealer, are you?), plus your availability for travel and/or research, you would appear to be suggesting an even more broadly based and highly populated scheme. A conspiracy, in fact, of the sort that James Bond tends to stumble over. Did you think to lay her low by laser? For a man in your position, the obvious display of wealth expended in the commission of a crime—furnishing the laboratory within the volcanic island's mountain, purchase of the submarine, all those armed and uniformed minions carried as "seasonal labor" on the corporate books—would be as bright red a flag to the police as the use of poison by a husband who had studied to be a doctor. Except for the small expenditures that would be possible to the common pocket—enough rope, for instance—keep your wealth as well on its shelf.

So much for your own schemes. Now, on to other elements of your letter. I notice you made only the barest of references to your two sisters-in-law, who, having been done out of their natural inheritance by your wife (would Lear be the family name, by any chance?), would be the second most obvious suspects to the police after your own self. Here, it would seem, awaits a ready-made diversion to dazzle the police mind; two attractive and hard-nosed upper-crust women, infuriating to the Columbo in every workaday cop, who could with only the most minimal effort be tailored to suit your crime. (I base my description of them on your description of them. Your comment that their disinheritance "forced" them to the same "cruel" fate as your own; i.e., "to marry money rather than make it." This gloss on your own history gives you rather too much of the benefit of the doubt, but never mind, never mind. In re your sisters-in-law, they would not have been disinherited were they not even more odious than your wife. Were they not attractive and hard-nosed and elitist, they would have been unlikely to succeed in the rather formidable task of marrying money. I detect something Gaboresque here, and we already know how a policeman and a Gabor are likely to affect one another.)

But you are uninterested in implicating a sister-in-law to dispatch a wife. Why? It is possible that you have for reasons of security or embarrassment neglected to mention an *affaire de coeur* with one of the sisters which would make her an inappropriate foil for your *affaire d'intérêt*, but I some-how doubt it. You already know what hell these Lear-Gabors mean for you; your next sentimental conjunction is likely to be a hell of quite a different stripe; an antifur activist, for instance, or an ex-nun. (Here I have revealed one reason for my own concentration on your problem; I fully expect repeat business.)

But I get ahead of your story. The issue at this moment is, Why not frame a sister-in-law? Easy, convenient, obvious, and pleasing to the police mind. The reason would appear to be only that your hatred of Blazes Boylan is so intense that you are determined that *he* will take your place in the dock (and on the seat over the cyanide capsule, too, if your state is one of those which still indulges *itself* in murder). He, and no other.

You detest Blazes, in fact, much more than you do your wife. Her you will be content to dispatch to a better world at a stroke; you don't even much care if she shuffles off this

25

mortal coil painlessly, like an ultimate visit to the dentist. Blazes you wish to harm, to mortify and to punish, as deeply as possible and for as long a time as possible. And why is that?

I suggest envy. Your "best friend" Blazes was born to a silver spoon, you to a McDonald's plastic stirrer. You have caught up with him, in some ways, but plainly you still feel inferior. You must pretend to be a businessman, but isn't your position a mere sinecure, purchased with your wife's money? Whereas Blazes, born to wealth, then went on to make "a considerable fortune," as you say, on his own. You belong to the same club, but do you, while within its ivied walls, *feel* that you belong? As much as Blazes does? Do you find yourself, at your tailor, modeling your appearance on his, and then are you privately humiliated and shamed at such apery? Was your automobile purchased either in imitation of his or in reaction to it (which is the same thing)? Do you find yourself just a bit inhibited in speech in his presence, both in your choice of subject matter and in your choice of words? Has he always been an exemplar to you, and have you always resented him for it?

And has he now, in the easy and contemptuous way in which he has usurped the wife you don't particularly want but very particularly need, gone that one step too far? Is *he* the subject of your perfect crime, rather than your wife, so that ridding yourself of her while retaining her money is merely lagniappe, the juicy by-product of your primary activity, being his total and permanent discomfiture? You needn't be embarrassed to admit this to me, nor to yourself, if it be true; clarity will be needed, if you are to succeed at your endeavor.

There is another point to be made, in this same area.

If revenge against Blazes Boylan for the ongoing insult of his very existence is in fact the primary motive here, then the joke will not be complete unless Blazes *knows* who did for him, and can't prove it. The best way to effect this happy result would be, of course, if he were present when you killed her—placing him at the scene of the crime—but you could prove that you were not. Having *seen* you there, Blazes would be very likely to squander all his energy trying to get oblivious policemen to believe him, when the story he would have to tell would be thoroughly without credibility from word one.

Let's see if we can arrange it. You say that Blazes *was* your best friend, that at the moment you are both—for your differing reasons—attempting to keep up at least the appearance of that close bond, and that you are more successful at the pretense than he. (Don't be surprised if he thinks *he's* the more successful dissembler.) I take it your friendship has revolved around the more usual manly pursuits common to successful and reasonably healthy men of such wealth: golf, perhaps tennis, sailing in temperate weather. You would probably think of hunting as somewhat too déclassé for your present situation, since I don't doubt that you are at all times affected by a prickly awareness of the distance you have traveled upward through the classes in this classless nation.

But what of shooting? Target shooting, in a building constructed for the purpose. The right gun club can lend a man as much cachet as the right racquet club. At once, then, join the most upper-class gun club it is within your social, economic, and geographic potential to join. In your seemingly casual (but actually quite strained) chats with Blazes, refer to this new enthusiasm, making sure to emphasize how many other important men you have rubbed elbows with there. If he doesn't himself suggest after a week or so that he join the club, you make the suggestion yourself; offer, with hearty camaraderie, to *put him up* for the club. Psychologically, he cannot refuse. He will join. You will shoot together. You now know that on the day you have selected, the criminological laboratory's tests *will* demonstrate that Blazes has recently fired a gun.

Part one is complete. It has been easy, enjoyable, and even utile, since your marksmanship will have improved since you have joined the gun club, and your marksmanship will soon be put to the test.

But first, as to that local inn, the one to which Blazes and your wife repair for their ongoing discussion of the Paphian mysteries. I know so little about it, save that it serves drinks in its bar, and would appear to have a large number of rooms: 1507 is not the number of a room in a *small* inn. Such a place surely has a restaurant as well, and elevators. You know of it; does it know of you? I think I can safely suggest not; it sounds a fairly large and anonymous place all in all, an inn that's more Holiday's than Mistress Quickly's.

However, the fact that the same room is always available for them every afternoon suggests that either Blazes or your wife has some connection with the management, either personally or through business. Since you mentioned no such connection, it is unlikely to be through your wife. So Blazes, I assume, is a good friend of the manager, perhaps, or alternatively he is a significant member of the combine of local businessmen who jointly own this blot on the landscape. Because of this influence of his, that same room is made available to him three times per week, is serviced by the maid upon his and your wife's departure, and is returned to the stock of available rooms, paper ribbon around the toilet seat and all, before your wife is seated across the dinner table from you at home.

You need a key to that room, or the inn's passkey. You will probably have to stay a night or two at the inn, and for this reason you will need a new identity. This is because you will have to pay for your room with a credit card, since cash is an anomaly today and you cannot afford anomalies. So you should get your new identity at once, even before you join the gun club, to give that person time to accumulate a paper existence.

There is nothing simpler to obtain than a false identity. First, choose a city in a state other than your own. Second, go to the library and look at the microfilms of that city's newspapers. What you are looking for is the obituary notice of a child born within a year of your birth who died before he was two. Sadly, the obituary pages of a large city will certainly provide what you need.

Next, you go to that city and rent a small apartment; for this, you can pay cash. Using that return address, and giving yourself the name of the dead infant, write to that state's Bureau of Vital Statistics and request a copy of your birth certificate; that is, the dead infant's birth certificate. When you receive it, use it to get a driver's license and Social Security card, explaining in both offices that you have lived abroad with your parents since you were a teenager. With driver's license and Social Security number in the new name—Minor DeMortis, let us say—you open a checking account in one bank and a savings account in another, depositing cash. You then apply for a gasoline company credit card and open two department store charge accounts, both of which will need no more than the bank references. With those, apply for normal credit cards. *Then,* at long last, you reserve a room at the inn in question, as Minor DeMortis.

Have you the patience for all this? There is little in your history to suggest any such thing. Before you begin this operation, ask yourself if you can really carry it through to the end. Of course, *until* the end, you will not have committed any major crimes—though a few minor ones, like the lies necessary to establish the new identity—so you can abandon the plot at any point if you decide you can live with your humiliation after all.

Assuming you have decided to go forward, let me tell you what to say when you phone the inn. You say you will arrive after eight P.M., and that you have been told by another traveler that Room 1507 has such-and-such a desirable feature; will it be available? (Plan B. If Room 1507 is not available, or if it has no desirable feature to which you can refer, or if you don't believe you can play that scene believably, you rent *any* room, lock yourself out with the key inside, and manage to get your hands briefly on the passkey when the security man comes to let you in. The soft plastic for the impression is in your palm.) (Plan C. If the security man merely gives you another copy of the key to *your* room, knock on the door of 1507 when the murder moment arrives and claim through the closed door to be the inn's manager, come to make certain the air conditioner won't blow up again.)

It will be necessary to alter your appearance somewhat when you are Minor. Don't do complicated, difficult, and time-consuming things like false noses. You must of course hide any really noticeable feature, like a saber scar on your cheek, but generally in disguise the less the better. A cane and slight limp, different hair style, spectacles, that sort of thing. And Minor will speak slowly and a bit artificially, since he's been out of the country for so long.

Whenever you are Minor, including alone in his apartment, maintain that façade.

Around now, it will be time for you to go to one of those pioneer states where any lout can buy a gun, and buy a gun.

And now you begin a correspondence between yourself and Minor. Minor writes first, explaining that he's just recently back in America after many years, and that your company has been suggested to him as something he might be interested in investing in. You respond, favorably. More correspondence continues, noted by your secretary. On the day that Minor stays at the inn, inform your secretary you're having lunch with the fellow.

That's the way you study Room 1507, to find the appropriate hiding place. The closet? The tub, behind the shower curtain? On the floor behind a sofa? Circumstances will decide. (If no hiding place at all presents itself, return to Plan C above.)

Eventually, the climactic day will come. Your secretary will have made reservations for you to take a morning flight to Minor's city, to stay at a hotel there, and to take another morning flight back tomorrow. You take the flight, you check into the hotel, and you immediately take the next flight home, proceed to the inn, enter unobserved (easy in a large public place), and secrete yourself in Room 1507 prior to Blazes's and your wife's arrival.

The point at which you reveal yourself to the scoundrels is up to you. Make it as dramatic as you wish. You may choose a moment which would lend itself to low comedy. Please yourself. In any event, emerge, show the gun in your gloved hand, announce you will kill them both. The idea here is to get each of them to verbally betray the other while pleading for their own miserable lives.

Having attained that satisfaction, you shoot your wife twice, in front of Blazes's horrified eyes. "And now you!" you announce. He begs, he pleads, he grovels. You permit yourself to be swayed. At last you agree, as emotionally as you can muster, that you must have been mad. "Give me the gun," he says. You hand it to him, spray him with Mace, drop the Mace can near your wife's body (it would be nice if it were hers anyway), and leave. (To facilitate your escape, it might be best to choose an entry moment when Blazes is entirely disrobed.)

Whether you hide in an unoccupied room (using your passkey copy) until pursuit leaves you in its wake, or make an immediate retreat would depend on the physical layout of the inn. (If you're up to it, it might be very nice to both enter and leave the inn disguised as a little old lady in a motorized wheelchair.) You return to the airport, take the evening flight to that other city, give yourself a hearty meal in a large bustling restaurant, pay with your own credit card, and return to the hotel, where you will find a great horde of policemen eager to talk to you.

Be truthful, within reason. Tell them you and your wife have not been getting along, that you knew about the affair with Blazes, that financial considerations kept you from leaving her, and that you cannot claim to be sorry that Blazes killed her. As to your own whereabouts, you and Minor DeMortis had a long and leisurely dinner here tonight and were probably eating your appetizers at the moment your wife was being killed by Blazes. The police, no doubt, will disbelieve you, but will have no excuse to take you in until they've checked your alibi. You assure them you will stay the night in this hotel, as planned, and fly home in the morning on the flight already reserved, where *of course* you will present yourself to the local constabulary. Eventually, they will leave. A few minutes later, so will you.

You must become Minor DeMortis before you leave the hotel room. Exit by the most unobtrusive egress and go to Minor's apartment, where the answering machine with which you have provided it will give you one or more messages from the police. Respond. The police will come to Minor's apartment. You (Minor) will be shocked by what they tell you, but of course you've never met the dead woman, and know her husband only slightly. "We've corresponded, and have now met twice." Yes, you two had dinner together, and yes, it was at such-and-such a restaurant and at such-and-such a time. After dinner, you both came to this apartment to discuss business, until the original you went off to your hotel.

If *you* were going to be put on trial, the Minor DeMortis flummery would fall apart, but you shall not be. Minor will make and sign a statement for the local police in one state, who will forward it to the local police in another state. The investigating officers will find all that correspondence in your business files. A background check on Minor DeMortis will prove him to be a solid-enough citizen, with no criminal record and no previous connection with you.

Over the next few weeks, you'll have to find time to become Minor DeMortis in his apartment every so often, during which intervals Minor will call the police to ask about further developments and wonder if he'll be called to testify anywhere. Minor will be very helpful, very forthcoming. Until, that is, the inevitable day when Blazes is indicted for

33

the murder of your wife. From that instant on, there will never again be any official interest in Minor DeMortis.

You will have alibied yourself. Except for Plan C, which I admit offends my artistic sense and which I therefore hope you will have no need to employ, I believe this scenario is certainly elegant enough for a scalawag like yourself.

FROM PETER LOVESEY

Sir,

You get an F from me, twice over. F for tact and F for accuracy. You have the effrontery to address me as your "dear friend." I am no friend of yours. I would rather rub noses with a Rottweiler. The alacrity with which you propose to murder your wife is depraved; your desire to frame your best friend is iniquitous; and your prose style is the pits.

Clearly, you are a megalomaniac. You need help from a psychiatrist, not a bunch of mystery writers. But I know as sure as death and taxes that you will ignore this sensible advice. It is symptomatic of your condition that you will ignore everything I say about the state of your mind. I am at liberty to call you all the names in my thesaurus (which is just as big as yours), but out of mercy to anyone else obliged to read these pages I'll settle for psychopath, degenerate, and slubberdegullion. I like *slubberdegullion*. I know nothing will dissuade you from your murderous purpose because you are impenetrable. You are manifestly crazy, dangerous, and a menace to society. You have one saving grace, and that is why I shall respond to your invitation. You are filthy rich.

I have made inquiries. You are flush enough to pay me an annuity of let us say a million dollars for the rest of my life. I shall need at least as much to see me safe after collaborating with you in this homicidal enterprise. Naturally I have my plans for securing my freedom. They are secret and expensive. But you will presently see that your money will more than gratify your monstrous vanity. I can guarantee your reputation as the Mozart of murder.

The timely end I have devised for your wife meets all your megalomaniac criteria. By the way, all the great murderers in history have been megalomaniacs, so you need not be ashamed of the label. This is a murder of such intricate appeal and soaring artistry that by comparison Michelangelo's ceiling in the Sistine Chapel is a graffiti scrawl. I would like to mention here that I am not a megalomaniac myself, just the world's most ingenious plotter of murder mysteries.

I am about to deliver the proof.

This will be a unique, custom-designed crime, taking account of your circumstances and mental kinks. You will require the patience of a cigar-store Indian, the cool of the morgue, and the fixity of purpose of a high jumper on his last attempt, all of which I assume you possess.

To put this plot in context, I must tell you that my thinking derives from a study of the most engaging English murders of which we have knowledge. A supreme example was the method of George Joseph Smith, who gained some experience in dispatching wives, for he married three in the years 1912 to 1914—bigamously, one has to admit—and murdered them all by drowning. With a fine feel for alliteration, the press dubbed him the "Brides in the Bath" murderer. Isn't that charming? I am sure you will agree that your own entry in the *Murderer's Who's Who* must trip from the tongue in a phrase just as evocative. It will.

Smith's motive was profit. He found gullible women, dazzled them with his wit, married them, insured them, and killed them, all in a short time. He would bring home a cheap tin bathtub from the ironmonger's and playfully invite the lady to use it in his presence, then lift her legs so that she slid under the water and drowned. Downstairs, all that the landlady would hear was a sigh and the sound of wet arms sliding down the sides of the tub. Then Smith would play "Nearer My God to Thee" on the harmonium. The next day, he returned the bathtub to the ironmonger without paying for it. Touching, picturesque, and very much of its time.

You may wonder why such a cool customer was ever caught. The answer is that Smith was greedy. He used the method too often. The father of one of his victims read of another "accidental" drowning in the newspaper and alerted the police. I caution you now to use my method once only. That will be enough to ensure your reputation forever.

Had Smith been content to drown only one of his brides, he would never have met the hangman. At the trial, it required seven hours of testimony from the brilliant forensic pathologist Sir Bernard Spilsbury to convince the court that such a method of murder was feasible. To add to the sensational character of the proceedings, a demonstration was arranged. A volunteer (in a bathing costume) was immersed in a bath and her legs were lifted. She almost drowned. She had to be revived by artificial respiration. Yes, the case had many interesting features. Take note. The Brides in the Bath.

I shall confine myself to one other case history of all those that I have reviewed on your behalf. It occurred in

1949. Again, there are bathing connections, though less ablutionary in character, for this was the case of John George Haigh, known as the Acid Bath Murderer. If the appellation lacks the alliterative charm of Smith's, it makes up for it in the juxtaposition of the words: the cruel bite of acid with the pleasurable concept of a bath. Haigh's singular claim to immortality was his method of disposal. He kept a forty-gallon drum—the "bath"—in his backyard, lowered his victims into it, and poured sulfuric acid over them. Vitriolic behavior, literally. Eight altogether. Very little was left. He boasted to the police investigating the missing persons that proof of murder was impossible without a corpse. Inconveniently for Haigh, the forensic scientists decided to investigate the sludge at the bottom of the acid bath. John George Haigh learned too late that certain items are not soluble in sulfuric acid, namely human gallstones and false teeth.

At this point, I can imagine you are asking what in the name of Hades can be learned from the failures of George Joseph Smith and John George Haigh. What is this man Lovesey driving at?

It is this: each of those gentlemen had a flair for originality. The freshness of their methods ensured their immortality. The press encapsulated the character of the crimes in never-to-be-forgotten epithets—the *Brides in the Bath* and the *Acid Bath Case*. Anyone wishing to secure his reputation as a murderer must take account of the public relations side of the business. You want a method that can be summed up in a pithy, evocative phrase. I have it for you.

The Jellyfish in the Jacuzzi.

Like it?

How could you fail to like it? It is the ad man's dream—the sublime catch phrase, whimsical and instantly imprinted on the brain. It has poetry, balance, alliteration, up-to-date-ness, and, above all, a striking image. The phrase alone is worth a million dollars.

This will be *your* case, *your* unique method of murder, to be spoken of with awe forevermore. "What a concept!" they will say. "The Jellyfish in the Jacuzzi. No one will ever think of anything so bizarre. The man was a genius."

And I haven't begun to unfold the beautiful plot. Not least among its merits is that there will be no mess—unlike the woodchipper method that took your fancy.

First, let me satisfy your curiosity. The Jacuzzi is your own, located, as you know, in its own room adjacent to the terrace at the rear of your house.

Now for the Jellyfish. I shall give it a capital letter, for it is a main character in the plot. To a zoologist, our Jellyfish is known as *Chironex fleckeri,* to the layman, as the sea wasp. If you have a modicum of intelligence, you will have gathered that the creature is known for its sting. So dangerous is the venom that beefy Australian lifeguards can be seen on the beaches of Queensland slipping on their pantyhose before venturing into the surf where the sea wasp lurks. A brush with its tentacles will result in an agonizing death within ten minutes. A woman blessed with relatively hairless skin is unlikely to suffer much longer than five minutes.

I had better describe what happens. The full-grown sea wasp has a body about the size of a melon, but box-shaped, with pedata on each of its four edges, from which hang the ribbonlike tentacles. An adult specimen may have as many as sixty of these, capable of extending up to nine feet in length, although retracted they are as short as three inches. Usually when a swimmer comes into contact with a sea wasp, the limbs become swiftly entangled in the tentacles. The pain is excruciating and the victim thrashes about, becoming more and more inextricably entwined. The muscular activity increases the absorption of the venom. Breathing becomes difficult, and presently impossible.

I trust you are getting the picture. As a character in our plot the Jellyfish commends itself, does it not? In the water, even in still, clear water, a sea wasp is practically invisible. It has a transparent, faintly milky appearance with a bluish tinge where the tentacles join the pedalia. Can you picture one already in your Jacuzzi? Certainly you may picture it, but you would be most unlikely to see it against the blue-green of the unit, even if you knew it was there. A water temperature around 80°F, by the way, is ideal. As creatures from the tropical seas, they do like it warm.

To save you rushing to your encyclopedia to learn where you may acquire such a desirable ally, let me give you its habitat. The sea wasp patrols the coastal waters of the Southern Pacific—Japan, South China, Vietnam, the Philippines, Malaysia, New Guinea, the Solomon Islands, Borneo, and the north of Australia. Deaths are regularly reported. In the warm months of October to April, many of the Queensland beaches are deserted because of the danger. There is a cruel Australian story of the English tourist deceived into thinking that the sea wasp was merely a flying insect; he was last seen swimming out to sea wearing a broad-brimmed hat for protection.

Money, you said, was no object in this murderous masterpiece, so I was considering the possibility of flying you out to Northern Australia to acquire the Jellyfish, but happily this will not be necessary. You can spend your money on my fees instead. I have learned of a remarkable research program being undertaken in the Center for Anesthetic Studies *in your town,* not more than three miles from your home. Scientists are attempting to produce artificially some highly specific anesthetics based on the chemistry of the venom produced by *Chironex fleckeri.* The research may well result in safer forms of anesthesia than any presently in use. However, for our purpose the most useful feature of the experiment is that the center has a room filled with 250 tanks, each containing an adult sea wasp. I have looked at the security there. It's a pushover.

So the essential elements in the plot are to hand (a protected hand, I suggest). Moreover, it has come to my attention that your wife is in the habit of using the Jacuzzi nightly, prior to retiring. Ten minutes in the churning water and she is pleasantly drowsy and ready for sleep. Am I right? I gather from your letter that other forms of pleasant nocturnal exercises are out.

The elements are there, like the pigments ranged on a palette. Any Sunday painter can use Leonardo's colors, but of course it isn't enough. You still require artistry, the sure hand of a master, to create a work of genius. As you specified, the crime has to be beautiful in construction, ingenious in practice, baroque in concept, and rich in detail. And you want to frame your best friend.

All this I am about to demonstrate. Give me your unswerving concentration, for I am ready to make the first mark on the canvas. You are privileged. Observe, watch it take shape and grow into a comprehensible image, apply your warped intelligence to the process and take delight in the brilliance of the concept. You may as well enjoy it. You're going to pay for it.

A first touch of the brush, then. A full six months before the Jellyfish is to go into the Jacuzzi, you let it be known

41

among your friends that you are taking up the sport of fresh-water fishing. Go to your nearest supplier and equip yourself with all the gear—rods, waders, nets, the lot. Buy several handbooks on angling and study them. Learn the basics. Three hours' drive from your home is a fishing lodge, a superior hotel adjacent to a river well stocked with fish. Book a weekend there and try your luck as a fisherman. If you catch anything, bring it home and freeze it.

Are you with me? These are the preparatory touches, blocking in the color, so to speak. Their relevance will not be apparent yet.

I propose to involve your friends in this adventure. It is likely that you belong to a set who take turns entertaining each other at home. At the first dinner party after you take up angling, you will give a present to your hostess. Instead of the usual flowers or chocolates, you will hand her a frozen fish. If you haven't actually caught one, you may buy a frozen trout, remove the packaging, and wrap it amateurishly, as if you had. You will, of course, claim it as your catch. Present it with pride. You will also make sure that your newfound delight in the rod and line is a topic of conversation. Like all anglers, you will bore everyone to distraction.

Next, you invite your old friend and fall guy, Blazes Boylan, on a fishing weekend. He is unlikely to refuse; after all, he doesn't want to make an enemy of you. If necessary, spice the invitation with the promise of gourmet eating at some of the excellent resturants in the neighborhood of the fishing lodge. Spend a relaxed weekend with dear old Blazes. At this stage I am setting you only one small assignment. I want you to acquire an imprint of his keys. He probably keeps them on a key ring in his trouser pocket.

This is how you do it. At the end of the day, you propose

a swim in the hotel's indoor pool. You change in the locker room, which is supervised by one of the hotel staff, who issues towels, bathing wraps, and wire baskets and assigns you a number. You and Blazes change and hand in the baskets containing your clothes for safekeeping. In the pocket of the bathing wrap, you will secrete a ball of Plasticine or Blu-Tak. You go out to the pool. Just before removing the wrap to take the plunge, you look at your wrist and reveal that you've forgotten to remove your Rolex watch. Tell Blazes you'll join him presently. Return to the locker room and give Blazes's number, and you will be handed his basket of clothes. Take out the keys, make imprints of his latchkey and his car key, pocket the Blu-Tak and the watch, and return the keys to his trousers and the basket to the hotel flunky. Next time you are in a town some distance from home you can go to a locksmith and get your duplicates made.

Don't be impatient. We are still several months from the Sting, and this is the time to familiarize yourself with the Center for Anesthetic Studies. It's attached to the Infirmary. Go between one and two in the afternoon. You'll discover that anyone who looks as if he belongs in the place can walk in unchallenged, but you might like to take the precaution of putting on a white coat and surgical gloves. Stacks of lab coats fresh from the laundry and packets of latex gloves are to be found in the storeroom in the basement below the main entrance. Use the elevator to the second floor and you will find yourself in the tank room where the Jellyfish are kept.

What a prospect that tank room is! Twelve rows of thermostatically heated, glass-fronted tanks, each with its silent inmate, pellucid, insubstantial, limp, yet utterly lethal. In an experiment in this very center, a solution of the toxin was diluted 10,000 times and still caused the death of a mouse before the syringe had been removed. Study the arrangement of the tanks and decide which one will be the easiest to plunder. You are unlikely to meet anyone in there. The staff enter the place only in the morning to administer the liquid feed and remove any specimens required by the lab. They scoop them out in buckets, which is what you will do when the time is right.

Meanwhile, let us apply some impasto to our canvas. The main outlines of the picture will soon begin to emerge. Another dinner party is in progress; it doesn't matter where. Once again, you are pontificating to your friends about piscatorial triumphs. The chime of the doorbell interrupts you. Your hostess is called to the front door, where—horror of horrors—she is confronted by an eight-foot shark. Thankfully dead. The deliveryman states that the shark was ordered to be sent to her address, with the message "You should have seen the one that got away." Everyone, of course, has abandoned the dinner table by now, and the joke is on you, a nicely executed practical joke. Sheepishly, you let them have their fun.

No one will guess that you fixed it yourself, any more than they will guess that you used the name of Boylan when you called the wholesaler from Blazes's apartment. But the call will be logged on his phone bill. And you will have quoted his credit card number to make the transaction. He won't notice it when the statement comes in. His ennui is such that he never examines the statements, but simply writes the checks. After all, he is so rich and bored, poor sucker, that he isn't interested in his outgoings.

You will have deduced, I'm sure, that you must have used the duplicate key to let yourself into Blazes's apartment to organize this coup. There, you will locate the credit card statements so that you can quote the number. But isn't it dangerous, you inquire? Mightn't Blazes return unexpectedly and find me there?

Not if you have the foresight to enter the apartment on a Monday, Wednesday, or Friday between 5:30 and 6:30 P.M., when he is pleasuring your wife in Room 1507 in another place. Neat, isn't it? Wear gloves, for obvious reasons, and while you are there, be sure to collect the following items: some hairs from his pillow, his hairbrush, or the inside of his hat; and a pair of sneakers.

Now for a master touch. A few weeks pass, and it is time to lift the enterprise dramatically into the public domain. You are to become the victim of another practical joke, a joke on the grand scale. It will be irresistible to the media.

You drive home from work one day to find an excited, good-humored crowd outside your house. Many of your friends are among them. Emerging from your car, you see the reason for their mirth—a huge, inflated plastic whale resting along your roof. With a sporting grin on your face, you enter the house and discover that your home has been transformed into an aquarium. All the furniture has been removed. Instead, the place is stacked with fish tanks. Exotic tropical fish, zebras, beacons, angels, Siamese fighters, damsels, rainbows, butterflies, puffers, Black Mollys, and Jack Dempseys inhabit your living room, your kitchen, bathroom, everywhere. Your swimming pool is stocked with trout. There are eels in the bathtub and sea horses in the hand basin. The press are taking pictures. Television cameras are pointed at you. Microphones are thrust into your face.

"What do you say about this, sir?"

"Do you agree that it's one terrific gag?"

"Who could have fixed this thing? Is it 'Candid Camera'?"

You assure them you have no clue who could have done it, except that any of your friends may have thought it up. You want to know what happened to your furniture. Someone tells you he saw it being loaded into a van and driven away.

You put on a brave show, smiling as well as you can.

In the middle of this, your wife will arrive home from her rendezvous with Blazes and undoubtedly turn hysterical. The press boys will love it. You support her and say it's beyond a joke. Whoever dreamed it up should have considered your wife's feelings. It's not very funny for a woman to find her home violated in this way. You put your arm protectively around her and pose for photographs. This is your opportunity to demonstrate your loyalty and affection to your wife. Be sure to make the most of it. I want to see you on the front page of every paper in America, the caring husband and the tearful wife, united, trying valiantly to put a good face on a cruel prank.

Everyone in the land will sympathize.

There will be intense speculation as to which of your friends could have pulled such an elaborate trick. You go through the motions of asking around, phoning everyone, including Blazes, and they all deny any knowledge of the stunt. You mention the earlier gag, with the shark, saying it must be the same practical joker at work. Even when a couple of vans arrive that evening to remove the fish and replace your furniture, you get no clues. The fish tanks were supplied by the main tropical fish dealer in the town. The removal people were given instructions by a firm that specializes in kissograms and hiring out fancy dress. They will say only that they were given telephone instructions by a man who wouldn't reveal his name. The stunt was paid for in advance in cash, delivered by post.

In reality, you made the arrangements from Blazes's apartment, using his phone. That's sufficient. Eventually, the police will trace the call to Blazes.

So we are coming to the final brush strokes, the highlights that characterize the masterpiece.

You announce to your wife that she is on your conscience. You bear an onerous responsibility for the ordeal she has been through. If you hadn't taken up fishing and bored your friends with it, this would never have happened. In compensation, you are going to give her the treat of her life. At the end of the month you are sending her on a Chocolate Binge, an entire weekend devoted to the celebration and consumption of chocolate. This lip-smacking orgy is held annually at a conference center a mere thirty minutes' drive from your home. She will check in on the Friday evening. You show her the brochure, having considerately first snipped out the information about fees and dates.

She will slaver at the prospect. As a woman of excessive appetites, she will drool at the idea of stuffing herself with chocolate. She can hardly bear to wait. And she will certainly broadcast her good fortune to all your friends. How gratifying—and what a generous, understanding husband you will seem in their eyes!

And now it's Stingtime!

A Friday. You rise early and set the thermostat on the Jacuzzi to a pleasant 80 degrees. You are taking a day off work to go fishing at the lodge. You have instructed the chauffeur to call for you at 8 A.M. You pack your gear, remembering to take with you certain items you will require: the sneakers you took from Blazes's apartment, a pair of latex gloves, a white coat, the duplicate keys you had made, and, in a polyethylene bag, the hairs you took from his pillow. Shortly before leaving, you go up to your wife's bedroom and tell her about the fishing trip. Inform her that you are spending the day at the lodge and you'll be back around midnight. You have arranged for the chauffeur to drive you home. Kiss her if you like—it will be the last time you have to do it—and wish her joy in her Chocolate Binge. Tell her you have called a taxi for her for 6:45 P.M., because the Binge will begin with a chocolate liqueur reception at 8 P.M.

You go off on your fishing expedition. It's a three-hour drive to the lodge, almost 150 miles, and you pass the time chatting pleasantly to the chauffeur. He is to spend the day as usual visiting his sister, who lives 5 miles further up the road. By 11 A.M., you are at the lodge, having a beer (only one) prior to going along the riverbank to find a spot to fish. Later, you return to the lodge for lunch, establishing your presence there.

About 2:30 P.M., you slip away and walk briskly through the woods by the secluded route to the local airport. You are carrying your bag of equipment. There are frequent flights and you take the 3 P.M., which gets you back to your home-town by 3:45. Walk to Blazes's private garage. It will take you about a half-hour. Put on the latex gloves you have with you. Change into the white lab coat and the pair of his sneakers you removed weeks ago from his apartment. Using your duplicate key, open his car. Start up and drive to the Center for Anesthetic Studies. Go calmly down to the basement, take the elevator up to the tank room, pick up one of the buckets stacked to your left, and scoop your chosen Jellyfish from its tank. Before leaving, take two of Blazes's hairs from their polyethylene bag and drop them into the empty tank. DNA analysis—"genetic fingerprinting," as it is known—will enable the forensic scientists to identify the hairs as Blazes's.

Convey the sea wasp downstairs, remove the lab coat, and cover the bucket with it. Then walk out to the car. Drive to your house, making sure you arrive no earlier than 5:10 P.M. By that time the maid will have left, and your wife will be on her way to the inn for her regular tryst with Blazes.

Let yourself in, deposit the Jellyfish in the Jacuzzi, scatter some more of Blazes's hairs on the water and around the edge, and leave a faint footprint on the white surround. Then drive back to Blazes's place, leave the car in the garage, and hide the bucket, gloves, sneakers, and white coat out of sight among the bits and pieces that are always to be found in such a place. Don't worry; the detectives will find them. They are very assiduous.

Then, of course, you must return to the airport and take the next available flight. There is one at 6 P.M. At the riverbank, pick up your fishing tackle and return to the fishing lodge for dinner at 7:30. The chauffeur will call for you at 9 and you will be home at midnight.

Meanwhile . . .

It's a crying shame you can't be there to see her drive off to the Binge, but it wouldn't do. You need your alibi. It's a pity you can't see her at the conference center—with eyes like silver-wrapped truffles—demanding to know which floor for the chockies. It's frustrating that you can't see her face when they tell her she's a whole week early, it is scheduled for the next weekend. No doubt she'll whip the brochure from her bag and brandish it at the receptionist until he points out that the details of the date and price of the Binge are missing. How she will curse you!

I dare say you can picture her coming home, flinging off her things, kicking the cat, going for the gin bottle, calling down the wrath of the gods on her wretched spouse. She may immerse herself in the Jacuzzi right away, or she may leave it till later. The timing is immaterial. As a creature of habit, she'll meet her destiny some time that evening.

And you will find the body and call the police and let them see how distressed you are.

The rest follows as surely as winter after the fall. The discovery of the sea wasp, the footprint, and the telltale hairs. The unraveling of the story of those increasingly sadistic practical jokes. The tracing of the phone calls and the credit card transaction. When the police come knocking at Blazes's door, he'll deny everything, of course. But the evidence will contradict him. The lab coat, sneakers, gloves, and bucket will be found hidden in his garage. They will learn that his car was used to transport the Jellyfish to your house. Someone will have seen it.

It will soon be apparent to the police that the sting wasn't intended for your wife, but for *you*. Blazes couldn't have known that your wife would get the date of the Binge wrong and return home that night. He had been led to believe that she'd gone away for the weekend.

The reason he wanted you out of the way is transparently clear. He was infatuated with your wife. He wanted her to live with him. Their regular philanderings are sure to come to light as the police investigate.

As for you, emulate the cigar-store Indian. And since you favor the writings of James Joyce, mark well what he wrote in *A Portrait of the Artist as a Young Man:* "The artist, like the God of the creation, remains within or behind or beyond or above his handiwork, invisible, refined out of existence, indifferent, paring his fingernails."

My scenario is complete. "A crime so beautiful in construction and so ingenious in practice that it aspires to the condition of art."

How could you resist it?

FROM TONY HILLERMAN

DEAR FRIEND:

I accept your assignment. In the following pages you will find my formula for solving your problem. It will leave you secure from any criminal penalties, happy in the knowledge that you have punished your faithless friend, and confident of posthumous fame as the fellow who committed a truly notorious, flamboyant, and heinous crime and got away with it. If you follow my instructions your only inconvenience will be a night spent in jail, perhaps two nights if your city is served by a slow-moving or slow-witted coroner.

But before we get to that, I will address your philosophical point.

I agree with your complaint. Crime in our republic has indeed suffered a serious decline. If you have noticed it in the effete East, consider how much more galling this condition must be to us Rocky Mountain Westerners. Lacking ballet, literacy, major league baseball, and the other daintier pastimes, we had built our culture principally on larceny and homicide, stealing all the states west of the eighty-third meridian from their previous owners, shooting the inhabitants thereof, and then, when that supply was exhausted, shooting one another. Our banditos—from Black Jack Ketchum to Butch Cassidy—were giants in the land. Even our lawmen, I point to Wyatt Earp and the infamous Sheriff Brady of the Lincoln County War as notable examples, were often criminal enough to warrant hanging.

Alas, that was yesterday. Today, as your complaint notes, we can boast only of quantity. My own smallish city, Albuquerque, tallied fifty-two bank robberies last year—so many that the gunmen were reduced to robbing the same places two or three times. Not one of these felonies showed the slightest sign of originality or imagination. Nor were any of those elements applied by the police. The only arrests made recently were of a robber who used a bicycle as his escape vehicle and wasn't very good at it and another who parked at the drive-up window, handed the teller his note demanding money, and waited patiently until the police came to lead him away. The once proud Federal Bureau of Investigation, formed in large part to protect our banks back in the halcyon days of John Dillinger and Pretty Boy Floyd, was finally stirred from its lethargy. To what end? It issued a press statement criticizing bank security systems, then went back to investigating librarians whom it suspects of checking out subversive books to Democrats.

In defense of the FBI, and real policemen too, it should be said that the sort of crime we have been offering hardly inspires the gendarmes. Thus I am pleased to join in your effort to uplift the genre.

Here is the way your murder will work:

You will call the 911 number, tell the operator that you have drowned your wife in the bathtub, provide your name and address, and wait for the police to arrive. When they do, you will show them into the bathroom where your wife will be floating face down, nude, in the tub. You will explain that you had arrived home, noticed that your wife was in the bathroom, and took advantage of her occupation to make a quick search of her desk because of your suspicions that she was having an affair with a friend of yours. In this search, you turned up a draft of a prenuptial contract which confirmed your fears that she planned to leave you. Thereupon, insane with jealous rage, you rushed into the bath, grabbed your wife by the neck, and held her head under water. Finally you noticed she was limp and still. You recovered your senses, felt instant remorse, and called the police. Now you are ready to pay the penalty for your crime.

At this point you must think that I am about to disappoint you, that this is no perfect crime. This scenario is typical of today's low standards—just what the bored police have come to expect.

Exactly! That is exactly the impression we wish to make and to maintain.

Unfortunately, you will now have to endure the only unpleasantness of this project—but only briefly. Your rights will be read to you and you will be led away, taken downtown in a police car, fingerprinted, officially booked, allowed to call your attorney, and put in a holding cell until he arrives. We might do all this in the morning, thereby allowing enough hours to get you bonded out before the judges quit for the day. But that creates other problems with our conspiracy. Best we do it in the evening. A night in jail won't kill you, if you'll allow the pun. Take along something to read. A few novels by this author (and properly noted by title and publisher in your memoirs) would be a fitting nod to your mentor.

When your lawyer arrives, remember what Ben Franklin said of his ilk:

"God works wonders now and then;

"Behold! A lawyer, an honest man!"

Or John Keats, who suggested that lawyers should be "classed in the natural history of monsters."

In other words stop thinking of this fellow as a Wednesday golfing partner. Think of him as one of an incredible 725,000 predators admitted to the American bar—1 attorney for every 300 honest citizens, 1 wolf for every 300 sheep. Hardly enough lambs to go around, and I want you to keep that in mind. In other words, DO NOT CONFIDE IN THIS MAN. If you do, he is going to drop out of the case and that is going to make the prosecuting attorney suspicious. Why did he drop out when he can earn a fee, the prosecutor will ask himself. Because something funny is going on here. Your lawyer is an "officer of the court." Engaging him in your little conspiracy would be dangerous for him. Worse, it would be dangerous for you.

Tell your lawyer simply that you learned your wife was unfaithful to you. In your rage you killed her. You want him to tell the prosecuting attorney that you wish to plead guilty and pay the penalty. Convince your lawyer that you are remorseful. You need him to give that impression to the prosecutor.

Next comes the homicide detective, possibly accompanied by someone from the district attorney's office. After all, you are a prominent citizen and the victim is a wealthy member of your town's social elite. Expect some top-level attention, because by now this drama we have so carefully scripted is beginning to take some peculiar turns.

In the interrogation room, the questioning will go something like this. The detective will ask you to describe exactly, in detail, what happened last night. You will say: "Well, I lost my temper and I killed my wife. I burst into the bathroom and grabbed her by the neck and banged her head against the end of the tub and then held her face under the water until I noticed she was dead and then I released her and called the police."

Something like this will follow:

Detective: "Burst into the bathroom? Was the door locked?"

You: "Of course. She always locks the bathroom door."

Det.: "You tried the door and it was locked.?"

You: "Well, no. I guess I didn't. I was furious. In a rage. I just burst in. What difference does it make?"

(Of course, you and I know it makes a lot of difference. It is one of the ways we arouse the police interest we require.)

Det.: "Did your wife speak to you?"

You: "I didn't give her a chance."

Det.: "Did she struggle?"

You: "That surprised me. She didn't. I think maybe she was sitting in the tub dozing. And then, of course, I banged her head against the tub."

Det.: "Did you do anything to the door after that?"

You: "Do anything? What do you mean?"

Det.: "Like unlock it."

You: "No." (Look surprised.) "It was broken."

Det.: "Are you sure your wife always locked the door when she took a bath?"

You: (Wry laugh.) "She had some faults, God knows, but she was a very modest woman. She always locked the door."

Det.: "Well, she didn't this time. You broke the knob

catch but not the lock. So it wasn't locked. Do you know of anyone who might have a reason to kill your wife?"

You: (Puzzled, fading into amazement.) "I don't understand."

Det.: "You say you wanted to kill her. Was there anyone else who might have done it if you didn't?"

You: (Laugh, shake your head.) "Well, maybe Blazes Boylan. My old friend. That's why I was so furious with her. I found out she had seduced him. Poor Blazes. She made him think she was going to marry him. When he found out it was just one of her little games he seemed very upset, as I was. It was just going too far, I thought. But I shouldn't have killed her."

Det.: "You didn't. But we will be needing to talk to you until we get this straightened out. So don't leave town."

I recommend some sort of a performance at this point—indications of amazement, all the appropriate questions, etc. And when your lawyer appears to escort you home (and establish his right to a fee by explaining things) be careful to pretend surprise when he tells you about it.

What he'll be telling you is what the autopsy showed. As you will very well know, the autopsy will show that the abrasion on your late wife's head was nonlethal and that she had no water in her lungs, because she was already dead when you hauled her in there, banged her head, and held her under water.

"What?" you'll ask. "A stroke? A heart attack? But why was the detective asking if anyone else might have wanted to kill her?" Your lawyer won't know, of course. And you must resist the temptation to even hint about poisoning. Certainly no hints about mushroom poisoning. Which is how you have done the dastardly deed. And don't ask me the name of those terrible mushrooms. There are more than one of them. You'll want the one that looks so much like that mushroom gourmets always fuss over at French restaurants. Check out one of the mushroom books at the library and look up the names. You're paying me for the plot (and little enough, I must say) and that doesn't include doing the donkey work.

Why mushrooms? Because there's a proper weirdness about them that fits your purpose. Because, as a former medical student, you still have connections and friends in the department of pharmacology and the department of neurology, where they are, respectively, growing the things and experimenting with their various effects on nervous systems. And because your wife fancies herself a gourmet, even though she could hardly tell that terrible Texas excuse for chili from the most deliciously subtle Hatch or Chimayo green. And because good old Blazes Boylan fancies himself not only an epicurean but a four-star chef. And finally, because you want a crime that will be memorable. What we're doing here will not only make the prosecuting attorney and the detective quickly lose interest in your admitted assault upon a corpse, it will send them baying and barking frantically up the wrong tree as soon as we point the wrong tree out to them.

I will pause at this juncture to make sure you understand the strategy behind stage one of this project.

Obviously the relationship into which you must enter with the detective and the prosecutor will be adversarial at the outset. Their conditioning will allow it to be no other way. When you present them with a wife not only murdered but wealthy, you present them yourself as their prey. How does one overcome that? By prepreempting their position.

"I am guilty," you tell them. "Do your duty. Hang me." But the conditioning remains. You are still the adversary. They will be happy, still, to prove you wrong. But now that means they must prove you innocent. The principle is a bit like that of the old-fashioned martial art we used to call judo—using the attacker's momentum against him, to throw him off balance.

So we wait for tomorrow and watch our plans bear fruit.

The detective will return with more questions—but now in the comfort of your home with a tea tray on the table and attitudes dramatically changed. The detective will be excited, possibly tense. The little domestic homicide you presented him has become part of something very, very big. Memorable. Exactly what you called for in your letter. Now he will want to know a lot more about what happened the past several days. And you will be happy to notice he is very curious about Blazes, your faithless former friend.

For this stage of the game, I recommend you appear to be slightly drunk. Not out of it, of course, but having had enough to relax the inhibitions, to lose caution, to speak more candidly than your own best interests would dictate. I recommend a half-empty shaker of martinis on the tea table and the smell of gin on your breath. But take only a single sip. You may need to be sharp.

Detective: "Thank you, no. I can't drink on duty."

You: "Some tea, then?" (Fill your martini glass. Take a sip. A small one.)

Detective: "Have you been informed of the cause of your wife's death?"

You: "No. I presumed a stroke. Or a heart attack. She sometimes complained of chest pains. But she wouldn't see a doctor."

60

Detective: (Looking surprised.) "You haven't seen the paper? Watched the TV news?"

You: "Not up to it."

Detective: "It was mushroom poisoning. Eighteen dead so far. Apparently they all came from the Yummie Yuppie Deli."

You: "The dead?"

Detective: "The mushrooms."

(I'm guessing at the number of victims, of course. It could be higher, but you didn't spread very many of the deadly ones in the mushroom display at the Yummie Yuppie Deli. Anyway, since it is an expensive ruling-class grocery and your victims will be Ivy League types, it doesn't take many to make a celebrated, historic murder case. It's not like gassing a Greyhound load of Blue Collars.)

You should display shock. Put down your glass with a clink. Remember that your face should register both the surprise of hearing information you didn't know and the shock of getting caught in your charade. The detective will have no doubt unraveled your cleverly disguised motive: that being a vain man with a notoriously unfaithful wife you saw more honor as a rich man convicted of a murder of passion (and soon released) than as a penniless wretch repeatedly called into the witness chair to publicly testify yet again to another of your wife's past affairs. You shouldn't have much to say during this exchange. Allow the detective to do the talking for you. Resist his theory at first and then allow him to comfort you with his version of the truth. This is the easy part. Now your face must show the shock of revelation—the mushrooms! As the detective unburdens you of your dark, humiliating secret, you begin to try to figure it out yourself. The detective's spadework will already have turned up Blazes

Boylan's name. So, with careful timing, drop in the connection, like so: "My God. Mushroom poisoning. But the only meal we ate out of the house in the last few days was at Blazes's."

Detective: "Blazes Boylan?"

You: "Yeah. Do you know him too?"

Detective: (Leaning forward, I'll wager, with considerable eagerness.) "Tell me about it."

And so, of course, you tell him about it. Not right away because you are almost, but not quite, incriminating yourself. But you gulp some more martini and let him bluff you into it. You tell it with every evidence of embarrassment and shame.

It seems, you tell the detective, that you had long since stopped loving your wife, a woman of voracious appetites and no warmth at all. But you needed her money. (If the detective doesn't already know this he soon would find out.) For several years it had been a marriage of convenience. Then, two months ago, she decided to add Blazes Boylan, your old friend, to her list of victims. She seduced him. Despite your warnings about her nature, he fell madly in love. Boylan came to you and asked you to divorce your wife so that he could marry her. (No, you weren't entirely candid when you first talked to the detective about this.) Nothing you could say would persuade him that she was toying with him. And so you said you would discuss it with her at the first opportunity.

(About here I recommend pouring youself another martini, but keep it small!)

When you told her that Boylan had fallen in love with her and asked her to let him down easily, she simply laughed. But about then her interest in him seemed to flag. Boylan noticed it, too. He asked you about it. You told him you hadn't a clue. Boylan said he would investigate. The next day he called you, very upset. He asked you to meet him at the club. When you got there he told you about Weldon McWeinie.

Detective: "Weldon McWho?"

You: "Weldon McWeinie, the famous Nobel Prize–winning Scottish poet, womanizer, bon vivant, and drunk. He is in the city doing poetry readings. Boylan said she had met him at some gathering of the elite, and McWeinie had made a play for her and now she was having an affair with the fellow."

Detective: "So?"

You: "Well, we talked about it."

Detective: "About what?"

You: "Blazes wanted to hit back at McWeinie."

Detective: "How?"

You: "Well, I said, why not invite him to some sort of party with some of the right people. People with manners. Let him show himself up. I understand he's a boorish fellow. Poets often are, you know."

Detective: "Like how?"

You: "How boorish? Remember Bernard Shaw said a gentleman was a man who knew how to play bagpipes but doesn't. Well, McWeinie does."

Detective: "No. I meant like how to show him up."

You: "Maybe bore everybody by playing bagpipes. Turn my wife off." (Take another small sip of martini.)

Detective: "What did you decide? And how the hell does any of this bear on a murder of eighteen people?"

You: "You see, Blazes loves to cook. He decided he would talk her into inviting McWeinie to a dinner at our place. He would cater the thing. Cook the fancy dish. Put something in McWeinie's portion to make him sick all over himself. He said that would be off-putting for her."

Detective: "Wait a minute. Why would he think she would go along with having this dinner?"

You: (Show of laughter recommended here.) "Blazes isn't very smart but he knew her. Entertaining her new boyfriend in front of her husband and her lover would be exactly what would appeal to her. And it did."

Detective: "And Blazes cooked mushrooms?"

You: "I don't know. I backed out. In fact, so did McWeinie. Blazes said McWeinie wasn't coming. But he was cooking a fancy meal for her and me anyway." (A shudder is recommended here.) "I can't stand seeing her at work on another man."

Detective: "Well, somebody fed her mushrooms. What do you know about that?"

You: (Thoughtfully, slightly drunk tone, another martini sip.) "Well, we talked about the mushrooms. I think I told him that some make you throw up. Some are totally lethal. I must have mentioned studying such things in medical school because he asked me about whether we had them in the lab there. And one thing led to another and—" (Hesitate. Look guilty.) "I finally made a call to the pharmacology people and got this friend of mine there to arrange for a visit."

Detective: "You went to the pharmacy lab. And someone showed you these poison mushrooms."

You: "Dr. Dottage, it was. An old professor of mine when I was a student. I told him Blazes was a mushroom gourmet and wanted to make sure he recognized the baddies."

Detective: "And Blazes took some of the poisonous ones?"

You: "Not that I know of. I certainly didn't see him take any."

Detective: "Could he have?"

You: "Well, yes. I suppose he could have snitched a few. While Dottage and I were recalling old times. I guess he could have slipped some into his pockets."

Detective: "We'll check."

Of course, you will have disposed of most of the mushrooms you picked up right under old Dottage's nearsighted eyes by sprinkling them into the mushroom display at the Yummie Yuppie Deli, saving only enough to cash in your wife and a bit of evidence to plant on Blazes. When the detective checks he will find mushroom soil and mushroom fragments in the left-side coat pocket of Boylan's jacket, exactly where you put the stuff. He will also find the sales slip from the Yummie Yuppie Deli, showing the purchase of a bunch of gourmet stuff DEFINITELY NOT INCLUDING MUSHROOMS, because you put it there. When he goes to the lab, old Dottage will remember Boylan being there and notice, sure enough, that some of his mushrooms have disappeared. I also recommend that you slip a copy of *The ABC Murders* open on Boylan's pillow to plant the notion with the detective that Blazes had got the idea there for hiding one motivated murder in a line of random ones. Detectives love such notions.

When the detective talks to McWeinie, what will the awful Scot say? He'll say: Yes, indeed, some fellow named Boylan called and invited him to a meal. He'd told the fellow to flit off. All of which is perfectly true, except that it was you calling, not Blazes.

What will Boylan say when the detective talks to him?

He'll say he didn't call McWeinie. He never heard of McWeinie. He didn't cook dinner for your wife. As a matter of fact, he will insist that during that entire period when you told the detective he was cooking this dinner, he was with you—seeing *Driving Miss Daisy* at the Paramount Theater. (You had arranged this, of course, to make absolutely sure he had no witness except you, and I hope you appreciate my sensitivity to your tastes in films. I could have as easily sent you to *Rocky V*.)

Is it necessary to pause here and instruct you on how to get the mushrooms inside your wife? I doubt it. Obviously it should be done on the cook's day off and, if you need a suggestion, try sprinkling a few bits and pieces on the salad you make for her. If you try soup, DO NOT overcook the mushrooms.

If you have any doubts about any of the above, it is probably about Boylan's motive. The detective has been offered a reason why Blazes would want to kill McWeinie (if a second reason is needed for bagpipers). But why would he want to kill your wife? We've offered him no clue to that.

Exactly! And be sure to keep it that way. If he asks, assure the man that you can't imagine. You haven't a clue. After all, he seemed to love the woman. And, despite the anger you described earlier, you find it hard to believe that he ever really thought she would leave you to marry him.

Why this strategy? Remember the thesis of your letter. If you and I (mere amateurs) suffer from the decline in the art of murder, think how much more frustrating it must be for the professional who lives with it every working hour. A bank robber fills out a loan application while biding his time to rob the teller's cage—and leaves it behind complete with correct name, address, and telephone number. Another bank robber hands the teller a note demanding all her cash. She says she can't hand it over without seeing some identification. He shows her his driver's license. Investigating officers called to check a burglarized business notice that the felons have dragged the safe up the street behind their car. The safe being heavy, the street being asphalt, tracks are left. The police follow the tracks to the driveway of the offenders' home. Not much fun in any of that for a dedicated detective. So let's give ours some small something to work on.

However, in the event years of dealing with brain-dead modern criminals has blunted his own intelligence, I enclose two "marriage contract forms" picked up at a local office/legal supply store. I've taken the liberty of typing the names of Blazes and your wife in the proper places (using a demonstration typewriter in the same store). You will notice that the proviso I typed in merges their estates upon their marriage, and that if the marriage is dissolved by either party, all property accrues to your wife. I recommend that you leave one copy atop her desk after you drag her into the bathroom and dump her into the tub. The other should be torn into tiny fragments (detectives love to reconstruct such documents) as if ripped apart in a rage. Deposit these fragments in Boylan's wastebasket when you pick him up for the movie.

Do I need say that my fee should be paid in cash?

FROM SARAH CAUDWELL

My Dear Tim,

*L*et me say, before we go any further, that I cannot hear of your committing a murder in the United States of America. It is, quite simply, out of the question.

You aspire not merely to murder but to Art, and in any work of art the choice of background is of critical importance. The background, in addition to having some intrinsic charm or interest of its own, should subtly echo those qualities of the main subject which the artist wishes to emphasize; it should supply those literary and historical allusions which are so essential to depth and resonance; but above all it should provide contrast, so that the main subject stands out against it as something striking and unusual. If one is painting a portrait of a beautiful young woman, one does not paint her as one of a group of similar young women.

I should be sorry to offend your patriotic sensibilities—but you do see, don't you, that the United States simply will not do? In a country where the homicides of a single day are too numerous to be fully reported on the television news—where every schoolchild expects a firearm for the next Christmas or birthday present—where minor disagreements between motorists are commonly resolved by an exchange of bullets—in such a country any murder, however interesting or bizarre its incidental features, is doomed to be essentially commonplace.

No, Tim, if you are to achieve distinction you must cross the Atlantic.

There are many places in continental Europe which would be, from the purely aesthetic point of view, satisfactory settings for murder. The peaceful and beautiful valley of the Loire, where the stones of such castles as Blois and Amboise are steeped in the blood of medieval intrigues—the great cities of Italy, whose streets seem haunted by the ghosts of masked and cloaked assassins with jeweled daggers in their hands—the dark hilltop overlooking the Aegean where Clytemnestra welcomed Agamemnon home from Troy—golden and murderous Mycenae.

To the novelist all these are almost irresistible. But you have a murder to commit, and one must be practical about it. You will have enough difficulties to face without the addition of possible linguistic problems. I propose, therefore, that you should commit your murder in England.

In England, despite the ravages of modernity, you will find an ample choice of appropriate picturesque locations and a social climate (at the time I write) in which the crime of murder is still thought of as uniquely extraordinary and terrible. You may also consider it an advantage that England does not have the death penalty. (I realize, of course, that even in your own country you, being white, well educated, and rich, are in practice exempt from so extreme a penalty; but in England there is not even a theoretical risk of it.)

Moreover, England is the birthplace of the classic murder mystery, in which murder is merely the starting point for a fascinating intellectual exercise and the corpse no more than a distasteful necessity. Yes, if you wish to achieve the status of a classic, an English background seems almost a sine qua non.

And yet. And yet. In spite of everything, is England quite the right place? Forgive me—Scotland is the country of my ancestors—will you think it is a sentimental prejudice on my part to claim that for a truly magnificent murder there is nowhere to compare with it?

I am not thinking only of the savage grandeur of the scenery, its dark glens and desolate moorlands, its somber mountains and unfathomed lochs. The murders of Scotland somehow seem to me to have a quality of drama and richness seldom if ever achieved south of the border. They are not, as English murders so often are, the casual result of some unconsidered impulse, but the fruit of some bitter passion long nursed in darkness under a reserved and dispassionate exterior.

No country to compare with Scotland, and no city to compare with Edinburgh.

A city one might almost think designed with deliberate purpose to symbolize the dichotomy between reason and passion, the light and dark aspects of the human psyche. Through it runs the long, deep cleft of Princes Street Gardens; on one side is the orderly decorum of the eighteenth century, wide streets and elegant squares, the quintessence of rationality; on the other the tenebrous wynds and narrow stairways of the old medieval town; and dominating all, the dark, majestic outline of the Castle and Cathedral.

Your crime, I need hardly say, must take place in the

autumn, at the time of the Edinburgh Festival. Artists from all over the world—dramatists, actors, composers, singers, and poets—will have gathered there to present their finest work to an international audience; and there you too will present your masterpiece. Surely you must find it irresistible.

And yet—is it possible, Tim, that you are becoming impatient with me? Do you feel that I have dwelt too long on the question of background when I ought rather to be advising you on such matters as weapons and alibis and untraceable poisons and other gadgetry of that sort? Are you even beginning to say that to commit murder in Edinburgh is simply too much trouble? Oh, I do hope not.

Of course, if you wanted to commit merely an ordinary, serviceable, workmanlike murder—if your only object was to bring about your wife's death and avoid detection—then there would be no need to go to all this trouble. Without stirring beyond your front door, you could arrange with no great difficulty one of the innumerable accidents which statistics show to be among the normal hazards of life in one's own home. Your wife could meet her death in the scullery or coal shed, dressed, I dare say, in unbecoming overalls and surrounded, poor woman, by all the sordid and trivial impedimenta of domesticity. But if that is all you want, then pray seek advice elsewhere—you are not the murderer I took you for.

You have said, let me remind you again, that you wish your murder to attain the status of art. How can you expect to achieve this if you are not prepared to take as much trouble over it as would be required for a novel or a great painting? *Ars longa, vita brevis.*

Every element of a work of art must be chosen with the

utmost care to contribute to the building of the final climax—
to what Aristotle would have called the catastrophe. This,
however, should be done with such skill—the great paradox
of art—that it appears to have required no skill at all: the
catastrophe should seem to flow naturally and necessarily
from the actions of the characters, their actions to be the
natural and necessary product of their attributes and circumstances. In truth, however, it is the artist who commands
their destiny—art has no place for the random and unin-
tended.

That is why a motiveless murder can never, in my view,
have any artistic merit, though sometimes, no doubt, it may
possess some incidental feature which creates an illusion of
artistry. You mention, for example, the crimes of Jack the
Ripper as having a certain appeal to your imagination; but
that is because they happened to take place against the back-
drop created by Sir Arthur Conan Doyle for Sherlock
Holmes. It is the Victorian gaslight, the mournful wailing of
foghorns on the Thames, the rattle of hansom cabs over
cobblestones, the burly figure of Inspector Lestrade in incompetent pursuit, which lend a mysterious and picturesque
quality to a series of crimes otherwise irredeemably banal.
To the murderer himself there is due, I fear, not even that
modest degree of credit which might be allowed to the ju-
dicious plagiarist—I suspect that there was no more art in
his choice of background than there is in a rock formation
which happens to look like a piece of sculpture.

A murder without a motive holds no more interest for
me than a novel without a plot. Indeed, it seems to me to
bear a close resemblance to one of those all too numerous
bundles of rambling and repetitious typescript which cir-

culate unsolicited from one publisher to another and are instantly perceived by even the most sympathetic reader to be utterly unpublishable.

Oh, I agree that the motiveless murderer may well escape detection, but that is hardly the point. If you were to be told in the last chapter of a detective story that the murder had been committed for no reason at all, would you applaud the author's skill in concealing the identity of the murderer? No—you would hurl the book across the room in justified indignation, resenting the time you had wasted in reading such fatuous stuff. And this, I must emphasize, not because such an ending is in some merely childish sense "cheating," but because it is altogether unsatisfying artistically: the climax does not develop from what has preceded it, and is therefore no climax at all.

Let us consider, then, the precise nature of the climax which you are seeking to achieve. It is not, in my opinion, the moment of your wife's death, though that must of necessity precede it. Nor is it the moment of Blazes's conviction for her murder, though that if all goes well will certainly follow. No, it is the moment at which he is discovered, by yourself and other witnesses, beside the dead body of your wife, with the fatal weapon in his hand. How is this to be done? I do not say that it will be easy—if it were, it would not be Art; but I will settle for nothing less.

The ideal, I feel bound to say, would be somehow to contrive that Blazes should indeed strike the final blow. Who is the greatest villain in literature? Iago. Does anyone doubt that morally he is guilty of the murder of Desdemona? No. Could any court of law convict him of it? No again. He is a true artist—the unseen director of the drama, not himself descending to the arena of physical action but inexorably propelling the other characters toward the fatal climax.

Do you think there is anything that would provoke Blazes to uncontrollable violence? You are his intimate friend—you should know, if anyone does, his secret fears and passions, the dark and hidden places of his mind. I do not know him and can do no more than speculate; but it occurs to me that many men are irrationally sensitive to any reflection on their virility.

Suppose you tell your wife of a conversation with Blazes in which (you say) he has half-admitted to having an affair with someone. You wonder artlessly who she can be and why he is being so secretive about her identity. Your wife will find this amusing. A few days later you mention a further conversation in which Blazes has hinted (you say) that his mistress is neither so young nor so attractive as he might wish, and that he is continuing the affair only until something better comes along. Your wife will find this less amusing.

When Blazes becomes impotent—you will not need to ask me, I imagine, why this should happen. You are trained, as you have mentioned, in pharmacology, and you drink with him sufficiently often to ensure a regular dosage of some otherwise harmless bromide.

When Blazes becomes impotent, your wife will attribute this to a waning of his desire for her: to the resentment of frustrated appetite will be added the rage of wounded vanity. On the first occasion, perhaps even the second and third, she will no doubt respond with sympathy and good humor— the most unreasonable of women could hardly do less; but unless you have given a most misleading account of her these are not qualities which she has in any abundance. A time will soon come, unless I am greatly mistaken, when she will up-braid his loss of manhood in the most bitter and wounding of terms. It is said that many men have committed murder in such circumstances.

And yet, I suppose, there must be many others who with equal provocation have nonetheless refrained. It may be that your friend Blazes, though American, could not so easily be persuaded to resort to violence—that there are indeed no circumstances in which you could rely on him to murder your wife. It is for you to judge—if you tell me that that is the case, then I will abandon the idea as a mere idle day-dream, and set about devising a more practical and realistic solution to your problem.

Very well. Your first step, clearly, must be to persuade your wife that she wishes to attend the Edinburgh Festival. I cannot think that you will have any great difficulty about this; she sounds to me very much the sort of woman who is, or at least would wish to be thought, a passionate lover of the arts. You are adept, I am sure, in matrimonial strategies; you will easily make her believe that it is she who has initiated the project and that you, in agreeing to it, are merely showing the indulgence to be expected of a devoted husband with no independent fortune.

Having set her heart on the expedition, she will naturally wish to be attended by both her husband and her lover—you may rely on her, therefore, to persuade Blazes to ac-company you. She may think it indiscreet to single him out, and therefore extend the invitation to several of your old friends; if so, on no account discourage them from accept-ing—it would be an excellent thing if you could make up a party of half a dozen or so.

An expedition of this kind can hardly be undertaken

on impulse. I am assuming that the project will be agreed on at least five or six months in advance, leaving you with ample time to make your other preparations.

The first of these is to acquire a tape recorder, of the smallest size compatible with efficiency and capable of being activated by sound. You will use this to record your wife's scream.

As to the cause of the scream I do not presume to advise you—you have been married to her for long enough to know whether a mouse in her bedroom, a cockroach in her kitchen, or a caterpillar in her salad is best calculated to produce a satisfactory result. Do please avoid, however, anything involving any element of physical pain or danger: I wish your wife to remain serene and happy, untroubled by any disquiet about what is going on around her.

Three or four months before the Festival you will find some pretext to fly to Europe on business. You will offer, with an air of good-humored martyrdom, to take the opportunity to go to Edinburgh and make the arrangements for your party's accommodation and entertainment.

I say with perfect confidence that Edinburgh will be an inspiration to you. You will walk down the Gallowgate, from the Castle to Holyrood Palace, and you will reflect on those great figures of the past who in centuries before have trodden the same path.

You will think of Deacon Brodie, respectable burgher by day, criminal by night—the inspiration for Stevenson's Dr. Jekyll. There is still a close which bears his name, for the city treasures his memory.

You will remember that this was the hunting ground of Burke and Hare, and you will think of their paymaster, Dr. Knox. Or do you perhaps believe the distinguished anatomist had felt no curiosity about the sudden improvement in the supply of young and healthy corpses for his dissecting table? I admit he was never charged with complicity. (The Scots have always had a high regard for medical science.)

You will think above all of young Lord Darnley, the husband of Mary, Queen of Scots, sitting at dinner with her in Holyrood, paying her charming and affectionate compliments, and knowing that in a few moments his fellow conspirators, armed with daggers, would burst into the room and murder her secretary Rizzio before her eyes. He had had other opportunities to murder Rizzio, and with a good deal less trouble to himself; but he was anxious that the event should take place in the presence of his young bride, six months with child, and in the circumstances most calculated to cause her terror.

Do you begin to understand what I mean about the particular flavor of the Scottish murder? With such examples to follow, your courage and resolution cannot fail you. But I must not allow you to spend all your time sightseeing— there is work to be done.

First you must find a suitable hotel—I do not only mean one which will satisfy your wife's no doubt exacting standards of comfort, though that is of course essential. It is also of crucial importance, however, that it should have two adjoining bedrooms, not obviously constituting a suite, with a ready means of private access from one to the other; a shared terrace or balcony would be very pleasing, but if this is unobtainable a connecting door of some kind will sufficiently answer our purpose. Ideally, I should also like them to have a good view of the Castle, though I suppose, if that proves impossible, that I cannot insist on it.

You will reserve these two rooms for yourself and your

wife, and another for Blazes on a different floor of the hotel. You will also indicate to the hotel management that on the last evening of your visit to the festival you intend to hold a rather elegant late-night supper party for about a dozen guests, and wish to reserve for that purpose one of the rooms in the same corridor as your bedroom.

The impression you should give is of a man of great wealth arranging a special treat for a wife to whom he is almost foolishly devoted. I am sure it is a role you will play with the utmost ease. You will make it clear that if your instructions are strictly adhered to you will be more than generous, but that any unauthorized departure from them will incur your deep displeasure.

You will go next to one of the shops in Princes Street which specialize in making traditional Scottish costume and order two sets of Scottish evening dress—kilt, plaid shawl, and traditional accessories—to be made in time for the Festival. One is for yourself, the other for Blazes—I assume that you know his measurements. I do hope, Tim, that you are not going to be difficult about this: the kilt is a magnificent garment, and I have no doubt that you will appear to advantage in it. It is not, however, on aesthetic grounds alone that I wish you to be wearing such a costume on the final evening: it is because the accessories include a dagger, known as the skene-dhu.

Be careful to show a great concern for authenticity, so that no sinister significance will be attached to your insisting on genuine daggers. The choice of tartan I leave to your discretion—if you have any Scottish ancestors, no doubt you will wish to honor them; but please make sure that it is of a predominantly dark color, with no white in it.

Finally, I should like you to make some friends of a kind

suitable to be invited to your supper party. They should be men of standing, whose word will carry some weight; but they must also be of convivial disposition, who can be relied on not to leave while the wine and whiskey are still flowing freely at your expense. Come provided with introductions to one or two of my learned friends at the Scottish Bar, and you will be sure of meeting the right sort of person.

Is there anything else to be done before you leave? Well, you will of course make sure of securing tickets for all the plays, concerts, and operas which your wife is anxious to attend—she is looking forward to them, and I should not like her to be disappointed. In the choice of entertainment it is right that her wishes should be paramount; but for the final evening I hope that you can guide her to a choice of something of artistic relevance. Perhaps a performance of Verdi's *Otello*?

Apart from that—no, I really think that is everything. You can return home with the consciousness of a task well done, and devote the summer to innocent recreation.

September, however, will find you in Edinburgh once more, accompanied by your wife and Blazes and perhaps other old friends, and surrounded by a glorious hubbub of creative enthusiasm. You will be moving quietly and modestly through noisy and gossiping groups of writers, directors, and composers, secretly cherishing the thought that none of their contributions to the Festival will be so original and daring as your own.

Initially, of course, the two adjoining rooms will be occupied by yourself and your wife. I fancy, however, that it will not be long before she and Blazes find some pretext for suggesting that you exchange rooms with him. You will good-naturedly comply.

Blazes may perhaps be surprised to find that the treats you have arranged for him include an evening costume in the traditional Scottish style, but will hardly be so ungracious as to refuse to wear it in public at least once. If, for some reason, he declines to wear it again, that is of no great consequence: it will have been sufficiently impressed on the minds of your intended witnesses that there are two daggers, one his, one yours.

On the last day—the day of the supper party—you will steal Blazes's dagger from his room. If in the evening he decides to wear his Scottish costume no doubt he will notice that it is missing; but he will hardly risk making you late for the opera by instituting a thorough search.

You yourself will of course be wearing your own Scottish costume, with your dagger prominently displayed. The stolen dagger will be secreted about your person.

Your wife, I have no doubt, can be counted on to be looking her very best for the occasion. I am hoping—I am almost sure—that she will have chosen to buy a new evening dress, something of richly colored velvet, designed to make her look just a little like Mary Queen of Scots. Yes, I am certain of it. And you, my dear Tim, will have thought it right to make her a present of jewelry to wear with it—let us say a necklace of rubies. Yes, rubies would be admirable. I realize, of course, that it will be her money which pays for them—but she will feel, as I do, that it is the thought that counts.

At the supper party she will look superb, her eyes still sparkling with the pleasure of the opera, her color a little heightened by champagne, the jewels on her snow-white bosom glowing in the candlelight, the unchallenged focus of admiration and desire. The evening will be a triumph for her, and surely she will not wish to linger while it dwindles into a masculine drinking session. Everything depends on her leaving before your other guests—she must not, she cannot do otherwise.

"Gentlemen," she says, "I must ask you to excuse me—I am a little tired, and tomorrow we have to travel." She bestows her final smile on Blazes—a subtle and shameless smile, assuring him that she is not in the least tired—and she is gone.

He can hardly follow her at once—you have portrayed him as a man of discretion. Refill everyone's glass—your guests must on no account feel that they have outstayed their welcome. Then say there is something you have forgotten to tell her about the arrangements for the morning, and excuse yourself for a few minutes.

You knock on the door of her bedroom. She admits you—why should she not? But if not, you still have your key to it. You say that you have come to say "Good night" to her. You throw aside your plaid cloak—don't forget that, it is of great importance—and you take her in your arms. Do not be tempted, though it is the last, to let your embrace be too long. While your mouth is still on hers you draw the dagger that you have stolen from Blazes—please don't get confused, you must use the one which has his fingerprints on it—and— There, the thing is done.

Now put her body on the bed. Arrange it so that the wound is not immediately obvious—so that by the dim light of the bedside lamp she looks as if she were merely sleeping. Or not even sleeping, but lying with her eyes closed in languorous contemplation of the lover whom she is awaiting. Hide the tape recorder in the folds of her dress and leave the dagger lying on the floor beside the bed.

82

Now set the tape recorder in such a way that—

No—no, first wash the blood from your hands. I cannot have your bloodstained fingerprints all over the room. I am, I must confess, a little worried about the blood—can you manage, do you think, to avoid getting any of it on the cuffs of your shirt? If not, you will have to take the risk of washing them, but whatever you do take care to use cold water—hot makes bloodstains irremovable. And do please be quick about all this—your guests will be embarrassed by too prolonged an absence.

Now make sure the door giving access to the adjoining room is unlocked and slightly ajar, and set the tape recorder in such a way that the scream will be heard—let us say, thirty seconds after the door is pushed open. You will, of course, have practiced doing this, so that there should be no difficulty about it. But you will remember, won't you, that speed is now of the essence?

Examine your appearance carefully in the bathroom mirror. Put on your plaid again, and arrange it in such a way as to conceal any bloodstains. Are you sure, quite sure, that your hands are clean? Very well then—you are ready to return to your guests.

It is possible that the next few minutes will be something of a strain on your nerves. You may perhaps become conscious that committing a murder is in some ways rather different from writing a novel or painting a picture. If you make a mistake, you cannot revise or repaint, or tear up your work and start all over again. And if you happen to find that you have mistaken your vocation, you cannot decide not to be a murderer after all.

But this is not the time to let your nerves get the better of you. More than ever now you must be the genial and generous host—it would never do for your guests to feel that you were weary of them, and depart before the drama reaches its conclusion.

Moreover, you must find some pretext to draw attention to the dagger you are wearing—I want everyone to remember that at this stage in the evening it was still in your possession. Perhaps you could guide the conversation toward the subject of traditional Scottish craftsmanship.

How long will Blazes remain among your guests? Not long, surely? When your wife is looking so beautiful and has smiled as she has at him, surely he will not keep her waiting long?

And once he leaves, the moment of climax is at hand. He will go first to his own room—he is too discreet to enter hers from the corridor. He will spend a few moments perhaps in attending to his appearance. Then he will go to the door giving access to your wife's room, and finding it ajar will enter. He will see her lying, as you left her, on the bed. He will approach and stretch out his hand to wake her. He will not understand what it is that is moist and warm on her breast.

Then there will be the scream.

You hear it in the supper room, and rise to your feet with a panic-stricken cry: "My God, that's my wife—what the hell's happening to her?" You rush from the room and down the corridor, your companions close at your heels—curiosity and good fellowship alike command it. You rattle the handle of the door to her room, frantically calling her name. But only for a moment—the key is already in your hand. You fling the door open and turn on the main lights.

There is Blazes, still utterly bewildered, his hands red with blood. Perhaps, in his confusion, he will have picked up the dagger, and still be holding it; but if he has not, no matter—it lies where he seems but an instant before to have dropped it. Framed in the window behind him—no, I am sorry, Tim, however difficult it may be I really cannot bear to do without it—framed in the window behind him is the floodlit outline of the Castle.

"Blazes," you cry, "Blazes, what have you done?"

You rush across the room and take your wife's body in your arms, brokenly murmuring her name. This is your opportunity to retrieve the tape recorder and remote control device. It will also explain any bloodstains which may afterwards be noticed on your clothing.

Your friends continue to look at Blazes with horror in their eyes.

And there we are. I hope I may claim without boasting to have provided the climax that I promised you. I do not know if you will find it as satisfying as you expected—you may perhaps discover that there is only one audience whose applause you really value, and that she is now incapable of appreciating your performance.

That, however, is not my concern—like other professional advice, mine is given without responsibility for the consequences.

FROM LAWRENCE BLOCK

*Y*ou think this is funny, don't you?

That's what's galling about this whole un-happy enterprise. You think it's amusing, with all your brittle patter, your happy horseshit about murder as an art form. Murder is never artistic and it is rarely formal. It is a means to an end. Almost invariably, it is a bad means to a bad end. An unamusing means, if you will, to an una-musing end.

Life, we are told, is a comedy to those who think, a tragedy to those who feel. You, sir, reveal yourself as one who does neither. You seem to crave applause for the artistry of your efforts at homicide while at once wanting to escape detection. If your crime should be perfect, if your wife should perish and your friend Blazes be blamed for her death, what-ever artistry you would purport to have displayed would in fact remain forever undisplayed. It is as if you would feed to the woodchipper not a human corpse but the good Bishop Berkeley's tree, the one that falls unheard, the one that makes no sound.

I submit, sir, that you do not wish to kill anyone, that you have not the slightest intention of harming either your wife or your friend. It is abundantly clear to me that you are not a man of action, that indeed the only decisive act of which you have been capable to date has consisted of marrying a wealthy woman and sponging off her all these years. (And, indeed, was that a decisive act on your part? Somehow I think not. Somehow I find myself suspecting that the decision was your wife's, that she saw in you a harmless and ineffectual toy husband, a perfect Ken to her Barbie. And who is to say she was wrong?)

You won't kill her. As it happens, your situation at present is ideal for all concerned, and not least of all for you. You have a rich wife and a life of leisure, and your friend Blazes has been decent enough to relieve you of the chore of satisfying the woman's carnal appetites. I would have to say that he seems too good to be true. Does he really cavort with her every other day? I can't imagine the extramarital affair that could sustain that pace for more than a few weeks. Indeed, by the time my reply reaches you the bloom may well be off the rose and the whole problem, such as it is, be a thing of the past.

Let us assume, however, that Keats might have been writing of these two, that ever will he love and she be fair. (Or unfair, as you would have it.) So what? I can't believe you really give a damn. Nothing you cherish is being wrested from you. The only discernible damage is to your self-esteem, and you prop that up by wanking yourself with the notion that you are going to kill her and see him hanged for it. All your plotting and scheming are not a preparation for action but an alternative thereto.

If you were going to do anything, you would have long since done it.

Infirm of purpose! Why are you wasting my time?

Of course, if you really wanted to do it, it wouldn't be all that hard to work something out.

Well. Here is what I would have you do.

First of all, I want you to contrive to enter that room at the inn on a Monday, Wednesday, or Friday at approximately 6:35, which is to say just minutes after your wife and her lover have quit the place. Have a small plastic bag and a pair of tweezers with you, and use the latter to introduce into the former as many body hairs, so to speak, as the bed linen will readily provide.

Your objective here is to provide yourself with specimens of hair from the more intimate reaches of Blazes Boylan's body. If his hairs and your wife's are readily distinguishable one from the other, take only his. If not, take everything and sort at leisure, with the aid of a microscope if needed. You do not want to linger in this room, not only because to lurk where they have lately lain is unsupportably perverse, but because you do not want your presence remarked.

This procedure should not be terribly difficult. One assumes the lovers are in the habit of showering after their dalliance, as an aid to concealment. Since they have a scant hour to spend together, they would be unlikely to squander more of it on a preliminary shower as well. There is, consequently, every likelihood that they will have loose hairs to leave behind, and that you will be able to separate them into his and hers, and retain his for future use. (I am assuming, of course, that the inn is not the sort of hot-sheet hovel where they change the sheets once a week, and where the mingled residue of a dozen or more ardent adulterers might coexist. If that is in fact the case, don't trouble to murder her and frame him; leave them alone and they'll die of tawdry.)

Enough. Having provided yourself with some of Boylan's hairs, you're ready for the next step. (Conversely, having failed to bring this off, you can abandon the whole silly business in safety.) But you say you've done it? You've harvested some hair, and have escaped detection? Good. Now go and find yourself a girl.

A woman, I suppose I ought to say. Though sexist language seems a small sin indeed compared to what's in the offing. Two weeks or so after you've tucked away a sample of Blazes Boylan's body hair, I want you to find yourself a woman not too dissimilar to your wife in age and physical type. They need not be dead ringers one for the other, but they could have the same color hair, they could be approximately the same height. If your wife is fair, fat, and forty, don't find yourself a gaunt, swarthy teenager.

Contrive to be in intimate surroundings with this woman on a Monday, Wednesday, or Friday between the hours of 5:30 and 6:30. A hotel or motel room—but not the inn where your wife and her lover do their sporting. The woman's apartment. Wherever.

It would be nice if you could bring this about on the afternoon of the day immediately preceding the full moon. Not absolutely critical, but nice.

Who should this woman be? That matters less than who she should not be, and she should absolutely not be anyone who could in any way be linked to you. For convenience she might be a prostitute, but surely not one you may have engaged in the past.

Yes, let's do it this way. Earlier in the day, you take a motel room. You pay cash, and you register under a name similar to the alias Blazes uses at the inn. (I assume he uses an alias, for security, and I assume that it's the same one each time, as it could hardly be otherwise.) You will have determined this alias somehow, and the name you use will be along the same lines. If he calls himself Roger D. Cole you might call yourself, say, Robert D. Collins. Or you might select a different name but use the same fabricated address, the same made-up license number.

Then arrange for an outcall masseuse to arrive at your door at, say, 5:30. Some of them describe themselves in their ads. Agencies offer a variety of physical types. I'm sure you'll be able to get someone who looks the part.

Shower before she gets there. You don't want to leave any of your own short-and-curlies in a compromising place. When she arrives, have her remove her clothes and do the same yourself. If the spirit moves you, have sex with her. But make it the safest possible sort of sex. You wouldn't want to catch anything from her, for heaven's sake, or to leave anything behind.

Then kill the bitch.

Well, what did you expect? Did you think I was just going to get you laid and send you home? Of course you're going to have to kill this woman. That's what she's for. She is to be the first and by no means the last, so by all means get on with it and make a good job of it.

The method is up to you. Let me say only that it should be quick and it should be quiet, not so much as to prevent her suffering—what do you care if she suffers? what do I care?—as to avoid attracting attention. Strangulation is good, perhaps with a homemade wire garrote brought along for the purpose. If you do this, leave the garrote behind.

If you stab her, carry the weapon off with you.

I suggest that you take her by surprise. You don't want her to cry out, and you certainly don't want her raking your face with her nails.

Once she's conveniently dead, there are, knowing you, two things you'll very likely feel you have to do. Neither ought to be necessary if you weren't such a wretch, but you are, so at least see that you do them in the right order. Throw up first, and then take the Valium.

Then you'll have to mutilate the corpse.

My apologies. I know this is distasteful to you, but there's no way around it. It's dramatic, and will catch the imagination of law enforcement personnel as well as journalists and the general public. There's no better attention grabber than a bit of chopping and cropping. You've already mentioned Jack the Ripper; I would simply remind you that it was the ripping that made his reputation, not the mere fact of serial homicide.

And how best to mutilate your victim? I can only point out that decapitation is unrivaled. There is something about a headless corpse—or, for that matter, a corpseless head—that takes hold of the imagination and just will not let go. Having severed the head, do something interesting with it. Stick it on a bedpost. Mount it on the dresser top like a wig stand. Hang it from the light pull.

"Having severed the head." That makes it sound easy, and you'll find out that it's not. You'll have to bring a tool of some sort, probably a handsaw of some size. If that's a prob-

lem, you might choose to forgo decapitation and stick to the mutilations that can be accomplished with a bolt cutter, say, or pruning shears, or a grapefruit knife.

It's your choice, you see. I only ask that what you do be quite horrible, and that there be method in it, and more than a touch of theater. Cutting off the hands, for example, is not bad. Cutting off the hands and leaving them folded over the lower abdomen, or arranged so that each cups a breast, is a considerable refinement.

You get the picture.

One thing more. Take a souvenir. What sort, you ask? Something small, I should think, and something the absence of which will not pass unremarked. A finger, a nipple, an ear—something you couldn't have picked up at K-Mart. Pop it in a Glad bag, truck it on home, and stash it in the freezer.

But you must not be solely a taker. Even as you take something away with you, so shall you leave something behind. Remember those hairs of Blazes's? You'll have brought them with you, and now you'll leave a few behind. Tuck one or two into her pubic mound, and leave another where they won't be likely to miss it. But for goodness sake don't deplete your whole store. You won't want to make another visit to the room where you are being repeatedly cuckolded—not now, not once the machinery of revenge is in motion—so you'll have to ration your supply.

Oh dear. Is the implication upsetting to you? Writing these lines, I fancied I could hear your sharp intake of breath and see the color drain from your face. I can't fathom why. Surely it has been obvious that you've killed this woman not so Boylan can be arrested for her murder but to establish a pattern, one which will ultimately be rounded off with the murder of your wife. One swallow, alas, does not make a

93

summer, and neither does one pointless macabre murder establish a pattern of serial homicide. As you stab or strangle, as you saw through bone and cartilage, as you select a toe or a nose for ritual removal, do so in the knowledge that you will be doing this again.

And again. And again.

First, though, you'll do nothing for a month.

By this I mean you'll take no direct action. What you will do, like it or not, is you'll spend the month living with what you've just done. At first you'll be consumed with fear that murder will out, that you'll be apprehended for your crime. And, I must admit, this is always a possibility. When I was a boy, I grew up secure in the knowledge that nobody gets away with murder. Since then I have come to realize the utter falsity of that statement; one comes closer to the truth by saying that everybody gets away with murder. Still, every once in a while a murderer does get caught, and you might be the one. Perhaps you'll have left a trail, perhaps someone recognized you when you checked into that motel, perhaps you left a fingerprint behind. Who knows what you'll do, especially under all the strain of first-time murder?

Ah, well. If they catch you, don't say a word—not a single goddamned word—and get a good lawyer.

They probably won't catch you, however. And fear will give way to guilt. How could you have done such a thing? What kind of person are you? How can you possibly live with yourself after what you've done?

These are all normal reactions, and you would be less a person if you did not have them. Perhaps the anticipation of these feelings will be enough to keep you from that initial act of murder. If so, I would call that a good thing. If you can predict your inability to stand the heat, you can stay out of the kitchen altogether.

But let's assume that you've done it, and now you're struggling to live with the guilt. Why, you'll find yourself wondering, have you slain an innocent stranger? Why could you not have acted directly against your guilty wife, whose murder would be so much less disturbing, so much less an occasion of guilt?

Don't you believe it. Although I can't claim much fondness for you, I assure you I have your best interests at heart. I want to make this as easy as possible on you and for you. Accordingly, I've planned a string of murders that will not only leave Boylan neatly framed but will also condition you so that the most difficult possible act, the murder of your wife, will not be undertaken until you yourself will have been so transformed by your actions that it will be easy for you.

And make no mistake about it, it will be harder to kill your wife than a stranger. You think otherwise because you have a motive for her death, and because you hate her and wish her ill. Emotions, however, are not such a simple matter. For example, you also love her. How could you not? If love were gone, you wouldn't hate her, wouldn't care if she had an affair with Boylan, wouldn't wish her dead. I could make a very persuasive case, my friend, suggesting that you have cast your wife and your best friend as the mother and father in your private little psychodrama. You are the little kid, locked out of the bedchamber while Mommy and Daddy are Doing Something Naughty. You want to punish them for leaving you out. All your fancy talk of artful murder doesn't obscure the fact that you're just a little boy, biting back tears at the bedroom door, heartbroken because you can't climb in bed with your parents.

I'm sorry. I'm not your therapist, am I? And you most assuredly don't want to hear all this.

Enough of psychology. Let us get back to murder. Artful murder, as you would have it. Murder most foul, I should call it, but I'll try to suspend judgment.

One lunar month after your first murder it will be time for your second. I shall not trouble to provide a scenario for this second crime except to say that it should be the same in certain particulars but different in others. Again, the victim should bear a superficial resemblance to your wife. Again, the act should take place between 5:30 and 6:30 P.M., at a time when your wife and her lover are taking pleasure (I presume) in one another's company. Again, employ the same murder method and use the very instrument for dismemberment that served to make a dog's breakfast of the first young lady. Make the same ritual cuts, carry the same souvenirs home with you, and, again, leave a few of Boylan's body hairs where they will do the most good.

Those are the points of similarity. Here are points where change is acceptable, even desirable: The woman may be a little older or a little younger, a bit more or less attractive. If your first victim was a prostitute, let your second be a civilian—or vice versa. You might, for example, want to stalk the shopping malls and supermarkets and follow likely prospects home until you find one who will be at home alone at the chosen hour. Carry a clipboard when you make your visit—no one turns away a man with a clipboard—and do your dirty work right there in her living room.

The second murder may be more difficult for you than the first. Your initial venture into homicide, you see, will have had about it an air of unreality. Even as you go through the motions, all the way up to the point of no return, you will be able to tell yourself that this is all just a game, a bit of harmless tentative acting out—and, should you abort it at the eleventh hour, that is in fact all it will prove to have been.

Once the deed is done, once Woman #1 sleeps with her ancestors, that story just won't hold up, will it? I presume you'll have come to terms with the guilt—otherwise there will be no second victim—but as you stalk your victim and make your approach to her, you'll know her fate and know equally how your role in her death will feel. You'll know what's involved in severing a head, for example. You'll know how it feels, and the sort of nightmares it will give you afterwards. Knowing all this, and knowing that you are going to go through with it, that you have in fact gone through with it once already, will make this second murder chillingly real all the way through.

At the same time, of course, it will be a little easier. And for the same reason—you've done it before. Thus you will be sustained by the knowledge that you are equal to this awful task. You have done it before and you can do it again.

Or you can abort it, just as you could have aborted the first murder, and that's an end to the whole thing. Your wife and your friend may continue forever with their abbreviated *cinq-à-sept* and you can resign yourself to being the ineffectual wimp you've been thus far. The single murder you committed will go forever unsolved, and you can sit up nights remembering every detail of the act, knowing that you could have gone on, that you could have ultimately included your wife in the roll of the dead. This knowledge may well be a comfort to you. *I could have killed her,* you will tell yourself. *But am I not a greater and more human person for having made the choice I did? I think so. I think, too, that I shall have another drink.*

There will be a third murder, and a fourth murder. We need not talk much about them, except to say that the same points of similarity will be repeated, while other aspects may vary just as the second killing varied from the first. Again, these killings will be at one-month intervals, taking place just before the full moon, except that they are not to occur on the weekend. If the lunar calendar would have you make your kill on a Saturday, do the deed a day early. If the moon points to a Sunday murder, put it off until Monday.

Why four killings? Well, we want to establish a definite pattern, and to generate enough local hue and cry so that the public will go a little bit crazy when a suspect turns up in the happy person of Blazes Boylan. I think, too, that four's a good number in that, having sliced and diced four women in as many months, you will have been tempered considerably by the process. You may not be Damascus steel, but I trust you'll hold an edge. When it's time to kill your wife, you'll be a dab hand at the business. You won't freeze up, won't be paralyzed by soul searching. The enormity of what you've done won't slow you down, because it will indeed be something you've done before. As a matter of fact, if you've managed to get this far, the next step will be quite easy. Killing, you see, is not all that hard for a killer—and by this point that's exactly what you'll be.

In fact, you may grow a little too fond of it.

Which could be something of a problem. I can see you now, seasoned by four murders, and looking forward to the final act, the murder of your unloving wife. *Wait a moment,* you'll say to yourself. *Perhaps I'm being too hasty here. Perhaps I haven't prepared enough. Wouldn't it be better to make matters doubly (or, more accurately, quintuply) sure, and put one more scalp on the old coup stick before tackling the Big Enchilada?*

If this thought comes to you, you must recognize it for what it is. You will not be playing it safe by taking this route, for in point of fact your risk of detection will rise sharply after the fourth homicide, as FBI profilers and serial murder specialists begin to draw a bead on you.

No, all this line of reasoning will indicate is a desire to postpone the end of your life as a killer. It may well be that you'll have reached a point where the game is everything and the goal nothing, where pleasure is to be found not in completing your original scheme but in tracking and killing someone once a month. In other words, perhaps you have found meaning in life as a serial killer.

If this should happen—and, farfetched as it seems to you today, I assure you it is well within the realm of the possible—I say, if this should happen, you must be perfectly resolute and must adopt one of two courses of action immediately. Either you must follow through as planned, making your wife your fifth and final victim, or you must forever abandon all plans to kill your wife and must change the pattern of your serial killing so as to avoid the very attention you have thus far been at pains to create.

(I won't go into detail as to how to manage this, but if murder turns out to be your metier you'll probably come up with ideas on your own. First send your ripper killer off into the sunset, performing killings #5 and #6 in a city a hundred miles distant, and #7 still further away in the same direction. Then let your killings from that point on be random in nature, in time of occurrence, and in type of victim. If you take pains not to repeat yourself, there's really no reason why you can't go on indefinitely without even creating the suspicion that a serial killer is at work.)

But let us assume that you will not be sidetracked by the prospect of a lifetime of bloody murder. You are going to stick to the plan. You will want your wife dead, and Boylan's neck on the block.

Fine. Nothing simpler.

On the day before the fifth full moon, the day when a fifth homicide is due to be performed, get into Boylan's house and stash whatever souvenirs you've accumulated from your four prior victims. Perishables you'll have kept in your own freezer. Now's the time to transfer them to Boylan's. If you've been collecting the panties of your victims, or odd bits of jewelry, or whatever, hide them in his house. Hide at least some of them in truly out-of-the-way places, where you can't imagine anyone would think to look for them. Someone will.

Include a link to the murder weapon. For example, if you've been improvising garrotes out of wire, leave a spool of that very wire in Boylan's hardware drawer. You get the picture.

At 5:30, contrive to be in the room where Blazes and your wife have spent so many happy hours together. Your wife will enter the room first. You will be waiting for her, hiding behind the door.

When she comes in, kill her.

Yes, just like that! There is no time to waste, no time even to let her know what's happening. That's part of why you've had to practice so much, so that you can now act decisively, without wasting an instant. Strike like a cobra, kill the bitch as you'd swat a fly, and then *lock the door*.

Now you've got time, though hardly a great deal of time. When Boylan arrives in a minute or two, he'll find the door bolted. This will confuse him. If he has his own key, the bolt will deny him entrance. If your wife has the room's sole key, he'll assume that she hasn't arrived. In either event, he'll remain outside while you do what has to be done.

And what is that? Ah, you must know the answer. You have to do whatever it is you've been doing all along, have to undress your victim, have to cut off such portions of her being as you've been in the habit of removing, have to set the stage even as you have set it four times already. However, you will not carry off any souvenirs, not this time.

Just how you extricate yourself from the room and how you leave Blazes Boylan will depend on circumstances, and may call for some improvisation on your part. If Blazes simply stands resolutely at the door, you might just unlock the door and stand aside. When he bursts into the room, surprise him from behind with a trustworthy blunt instrument, knocking him even more senseless than usual. Get a little of her blood on his hands and clothes, and you might consider slipping her nose, or whatever, into his jacket pocket. Then get out of there, and let him explain.

If you have to slip out the back door and leave Blazes out front, that's fine, too. I can't get hung up on technicalities, as they will vary with the precise nature of the premises where the murder is to take place, with which I'm unfamiliar, and with his behavior, which I cannot predict. No matter. You'll find a way out. And Boylan, once the trap is sprung, will not.

I don't think you'll do any of this, and I certainly don't think you'll do all of it. I don't think you've got the heart for it.

But if you do it, it'll work.

FROM TIM

DEAR FRIENDS,

F rankly, I was shocked by the five letters I received in response to my genteel query. Not shocked by the content; on that level, I was delighted, fascinated, even inspired. But, I am shocked by the contempt in which I seem to be held. I suppose everyone—even Vlad the Impaler, I would guess—wants to be loved. Love is not an emotion that binds me to much, however, so I would have settled for "admire" (perhaps with reservations) or "respect." Instead, it seems I must be content with the title "employer."

Commerce is not the most promising basis for a relationship, but it's a beginning. After reading the introductions to many of your suggested solutions, I sensed that some among you, perhaps, fancied me, say, a shit. I think as you get to know me, you may change your minds. I may seem a bit practiced or stilted in character, too polite, overly politic, but etiquette is an inscrutable mask—a necessity in this line of work. While I am not praised coast to coast for my skills at deipnosophy, I am said to be a withering conversationalist, capable of fingering the swollen pride of any of the pompous gits who inhabit my social stratum.

I can skewer most men because I have spent years studying them. I think I do a damn good imitation because I know well the condition of men, at least what passes for it. I can brag in a manner that annoys half those within earshot. I can spit to the curb. I can sit in an airplane and loudly discuss the intricacies of the strategic plan of my booming business. I can tell jokes to a friend while standing at a urinal in a baseball stadium. I can chew with my mouth open. I can describe the pleasure of blowing the head off a duck. I can argue that the rich don't make enough money, and later complain that the poor make too much. I can leave the company of an acquaintance on December 31st and say "See you next year" and then burst out laughing. I can assert that the media are to blame. I can smile so broadly that all my teeth show. I can have an opinion on any public issue and begin that opinion with a variation on the words, "It all depends on the context." I can find an urgent reason to use my portable telephone in a crowded public situation. I can toast a young woman and say, "Here's looking up your address." I can slap a back. I can leave the impression that I have spent the better part of my youth on a swift sloop mastering the techniques of sailing.

And I can listen to another man do any of the above and pretend to wear an expression of serene indifference.

My credentials are secure, then. It is my motive that some of you find unworthy. But doesn't every motive pale alongside the act itself? The revelation of the motive—in a good book or a bad newspaper—is always a disappointment. Murder is an occasion of splendid excess such that whatever circumstances drove one to it can never provide a successful accounting. If the motive did explain the act, it seems to me, then murder would hold no more interest than a barroom brawl—a great sport if you happen upon it in progress, but nothing to write about or even to contemplate.

Moreover, to consider my animal motive—mere revenge—without placing it in the context of art (to which I intend to raise it) is to whittle and pare my thinking so ruthlessly with Occam's razor that you wind up with a skeleton meant to resemble flesh. Haven't I indicated that this act should aspire to conditions far beyond the mundane? Reducing my intent to mere revenge is like arguing that Shakespeare wrote his plays to earn his pay from the Globe or that Michelangelo hauled his scaffolding to the basilica in order to win a few indulgences from the pope.

Since I first wrote each of you, the particulars of my life have not changed. The trysts still occur at the same place, same time—only the frequency has picked up. They meet *every* day now. My wife's desire and cruelty are fueled, it seems, by the same engine. You might think that I am equally cruel—given the nature of this correspondence—but even I draw a line in my treatment of those on this side of the Styx. I might kill someone but I would never purposefully injure another's feelings.

Cruelty in our age is difficult because so much of our lives have become an open book. And true cruelty requires the knowledge of another's secrets. Today, with everyone jabbering to everyone else about their private fears, addictions, sins, and thoughts, it becomes harder to locate that tender spot in which to insert the verbal dagger. The other day, my wife found a bull's-eye in the heart of a neighbor.

We had been invited to a friend's house for a dinner party and were seated at a table of ten. Blazes was there, of course. He seems to show up at the most unexpected places these days. I know that audacity is the trademark of such affairs, but I will confess that his presence in the same room wounds me more than the pornographic pictures that play on the screen of my imagination when I am alone in bed, moments from sleep. Such are my circumstances.

Also present at the dinner table was an innocent and altogether sympathetic couple, Georgia and Ben. Because of a peculiar seating arrangement, Georgia was sitting next to another woman, an old friend of hers. They were talking quietly to each other. Otherwise, the table was lively, all mouths running, laughter rushing up the mahogany walls to a conservatory ceiling of glass through which we beheld the stars. Then, as it happens, one of those peculiar silences swept the table. Scientists claim such moments arrive in standard conversation every seven or eleven minutes. You know what I am talking about—that uncomfortable moment when each raconteur arrives at the conclusion of an anecdote simultaneously and all the chattering evaporates at once. At our table, every speaker went silent, save one. The staccato puffs of laughter climbing the walls simply slid back down, revealing that one person who was still talking. Georgia. She was midway through a thought, a tender moment of giddy confession to her friend: ". . . and I am so lucky because Ben is not only a wonderful father and provider but a great lover."

Poor innocent Georgia. She was still speaking at a conversational volume. Her remark fell onto the table, naked, without context. For a moment, we all looked at her and smiles were about to sprout on our faces—at any other table, this would have been a comic accident—when my bride snapped, "No, he's not."

Is it possible to describe the savagery of this moment? Those three words seemed to still the winds out of doors. A menacing silence hunkered down upon the table. Everyone was acutely aware that if anyone at the table could possibly make such charges, it would be my wife. And therein lies the profound cruelty of the moment—not the adultery, but the realization that if my wife's rejoinder cast doubt on Ben's prowess as a man, it was certainly *true*.

I remember seeing Georgia's face contorted by a speechless horror. To have one's emotion violently jerked from playful delight to disgusting epiphany leaves the head frozen at a tilt and the face rippling with tics. I remember turning away from Georgia, out of respect and perhaps empathy, to see a strangely similar expression, albeit in a minor key, moving its way onto the countenance of Blazes. Perhaps it was his first encounter with her kind of cruelty. Perhaps he was thinking what I had come to know. One day, after everything had been worked out to his specifications, with me safely at a remove, he would be on the receiving end of one of my wife's impromptu observations.

The next day I realized that Blazes's specifications would never be fulfilled. I checked the mailbox I maintain under an assumed name and eagerly slit open the envelope from Mr. Westlake. Perhaps my mood was influenced by the brutality I had witnessed the night before. Whatever it was, I read this solution with such happiness that I concluded that there was no point waiting for the other letters to arrive. I immediately set myself to the task.

According to Mr. Westlake's instructions, I would need to create the life and times of another person in a nearby town. So, I located the right town and went to the local library to examine the obituaries. I found a great name listed on the exact birthday of my wife. I chose this poor child to be my alter ego, mainly because Diana Clement was a girl.

Given my physique, my smooth hairless face, and my androgynous features, I am occasionally mistaken for a woman. This solution offered me the role of a lifetime. I obtained Diana's birth certificate. (Sure enough, births are not correlated with deaths at the recordkeeping department. This business seems too easy.) After a few experiments in cross-dressing, I realized that my transition from me to Diana required only that I carry three things in my unisex throw bag (J. Crew, $29.95, I recommend the Dijon color): a wig, a padded brassiere, and a pair of expensive pumps.

My transformation took only five minutes. I would wear a button-down-collar shirt, perfectly masculine. But, insert a modest bosom, and you have a casual blouse à-la J. C. Penney, and seen from nine to five every weekday all over America. A pair of casual men's slacks possesses the same office-attire ambiguity. This leaves the head and the feet.

Women's wigs are realistic looking; the technology appears to be years ahead of toupees. The difference can be traced to the fact that women's hair styles don't necessarily entail a part. (Since all hairpieces—for men or for women—need to be partless, many wigs for women look natural. Yet, when anyone sees an arch of styled hair tracing a curve from ear to ear on a man, the first thought is, rug.) Finally, as to the feet, nothing feminizes a body like a pair of $500 pumps. You may quote me.

The beauty part is this: As a man, I slip into an unattended women's restroom. Five minutes later, I exit with a bit of sashay to my step, a touch of makeup and lipstick on my face, and a voice modulated up the register (no problem for this tenor). I can even suppress my manly smile, coylike, to create a different face for me as a woman. I am a rather plain, almost tough, looking woman with long brown hair. But, add a bit of flirtation, and nearly any man will suddenly think of me as attractive. My transformation is complete. I am Diana.

The ease of such a change makes me wonder what a Sherlock Holmes would write about in contemporary America. Only 150 years ago, he was regularly publishing monographs proving a direct correspondence between a man's cigar ash and his neighborhood in London or a woman's taste in silk handkerchiefs and her station. Today he would have to forget writing about differences in class or address; he'd be lucky if the differences between all men's and women's appearances would fill his notebook.

My enthusiasm for this ruse provoked me to test it. As Diana, I have taken some clothing to a local dry cleaner, and become acquainted with the proprietor, a pleasant man. Over time, I arrived at a theory one could only formulate after extensive experience at transvestism: People come to recognize the features of a person not by their simple appearance but by the personality that animates them. Change the personality and you have a different look. To prove this, I entered the shop as a man. I was two inches shorter than Diana, had short red hair, my smile pulled back somewhat pretentiously at the corners, and I had about me the mildly disdainful air that most take as a sign of wealth. My shopkeeper never gave me a second look. He answered my request for directions and sent me away. A few days later, when Diana showed up, he was all hands and loud hellos.

I simply had too much fun in this role, getting credit cards and applying for various licenses. I realize the psychoanalysts will have a field day with this part of the auto-biography, but so what, I'll happily give them something to do. I won't tell all the stories. Suffice it to say that a summer-stock version of *M. Butterfly* was nearly played out at the local motor vehicle department between Diana and a young pa-trolman eager to reveal to me the mysteries of parallel park-ing and the three-point turn.

Much of the pleasure of creating another character de-rives from the improvisation needed to project a distinct personality. To assist in this I had come up with an invention that allows Diana to return her phone calls—promptly if need be—seven days a week, twenty-four hours a day. At Diana's apartment, I installed an answering machine, the kind you can call from another phone to hear your recorded messages. But this machine is itself wired to a modem (Radio Shack, $100). After the machine records an incoming mes-sage, the modem is programmed to wait five minutes and then dial a certain 800 number. That phone number is my private beeper, a common item among those like myself who strive to maintain the appearance of active employment. Thus, five minutes after every phone call to Diana, I receive a beep. I check the machine. If it is important—and every phone call is when you are creating a character—I call back. (In the end, I can simply deprogram the modem—and since local phone companies don't keep records of 800 phone calls, all evidence will disappear.) Needless to say, Diana maintains a low profile with the major players of her neighborhood—people who might want to know too much—but is already well known to the supernumeraries—the dry cleaner, the grocer, the video shop operator. The perfect fake identity for the perfect murder.

Content in the accomplishment of creating Diana's tidy

world, I was ready to move on to the next step when Mr. Lovesey's note arrived. Now, here was a rococo approach, touched up with flourishes of the bizarre—a shark answering the front door. I threw myself into the scheme.

I would need keys, car keys, house keys, the passkey to the inn. I feared this kind of labor at first. This is the kind of chancey spadework that makes the heart pound because it demands a degree of pluck lacking in most of us. I found it great exercise and a necessary preparation for the most brazen act of all.

To wear sheer confidence on one's face is to conquer the world. For those of you warming up to admonish me about the dangers of arrogance and hubris, set down your pens. Overconfidence is a flaw, but confidence is a must. A confident man checks himself constantly, always keeping himself well within the range of his own talents. I was stunned how much will fall in the direction you want it simply by *willing* it to do so. The world is populated by hesitant men and women, anxiously awaiting their instructions. The world is open to those who unabashedly issue them.

At an out-of-town club full of old friends, to which Blazes and I had been invited, I realized I had my chance. I arranged for Blazes and me to travel in his car. Valet parking insists you keep your keys in the car. During lunch, I excused myself to go table-hopping. I said I would return in ten minutes. I walked straight to the parking lot and ordered the valet to bring around "the car." Having seen me arrive in it, he simply assumed the car to be mine. I then drove it to an out-of-the-way locksmith (previously scoped out), had the car and house keys copied, and returned in well under ten minutes. The valet parked the car. On the way out of the club, to keep everyone's suspicions in check, I made an excuse with Blazes to drive his car—something about some interesting houses I wanted to show him, would he mind if I drove? The valet was not at all surprised when I took command of the conversation out front and said, as if I were the owner, "Bring around the Lincoln."

Of course, keys are but a minor part of this solution. Mr. Lovesey demands that I be a fisherman, which thankfully I am. Now, however, I had to make a spectacle of it. I invited a few guys on fishing expeditions. I bought the best equipment. I subscribed to *Cut Bait Magazine*. I began to exaggerate my catches. But after establishing this groundwork, Mr. Lovesey's solution calls for a number of devilish pranks. I wanted to come up with my own. Granted, one shouldn't overplay a bit like this, but let me be the first to say, and I probably am: Keys are easy, seafood is hard.

My acquaintance with the curator of the marine laboratory allowed me to know—all artfully overheard—that something extraordinary was soon due at the docks: two dozen *Macrocheira kaempferi,* the famous giant crabs of Japan. The big boys of this breed boast a chela-span of twelve to thirteen feet. Yes, *feet.* Long spidery critters, each with a dorsal housing about a foot in diameter from which radiates ten emaciated periopods or walking legs, each with the bore of, say, your index finger and capable of lifting the animal's shell three to four feet in the air.

Transportation was crucial to my purpose, and this is where it helps being a man. Everyone has an acquaintance who maintains a collection of curious contacts, the fellow who whispers to you after a third bourbon, during a moment of ersatz camaraderie, that he knows a man to call when you need *real* work done. Your pal's eyes widen and he gives you that conspiratorial click out the side of his cheek, meant to suggest that this is the kind of information just us serious men need to know and, by golly, he's just one of those serious men.

I remembered the name of the fixer mentioned during one of these conversations, and one afternoon I paid a call. He operates out of a window. You don't see him; he doesn't see you. I got in the line with the crackheads and the penniless whores submitting their résumés. I whispered my request: Steal a number of large, unguarded crates at the pier; at 6 A.M. drive them to a particular address (my own) and release the contents—a dozen large but harmless crabs— onto the lawn. The fixer asked a few questions of logistics— never suggesting that this request was any stranger than the last one he'd taken—and he named his price. I handed the money through the window and gave him the date of arrival.

On the appointed morning, the men delivered and unpacked the crates without a trace. Around dawn, about ten minutes of six, the phone rang. My wife, as usual, answered it. The neighbor called to suggest strongly that we look out to our front lawn. My wife ran down to my room shouting that something freakish was going on. I ran to my window to see what was the matter. And what before my wondrous eyes did appear? But . . . a scene that would frighten Dante. The crabs were only now beginning to stir from the lethargy of crate lag. Most of them were scratching their way across the yard, leaving alien glyphs in the grass. One had apparently died and stiffened en route, so the men had ingeniously suspended him from a tree branch by one claw. A nice touch. Another had made it to the driveway and was posting toward the street. I rapped on the window (although I kept up a face of alarm for my wife's benefit, I also wanted to appear in possession of normal male curiosity). My wife and I both moved toward the window to get a better look: Two dozen eighteen-inch stalks topped with eyes like black dimes looked frantically in all directions. Scores of aimless claws wagged menacingly in the air with a clicking hiss.

The entire scene couldn't have been more effective. And the serendipitous appearance of the dead crab creaking on the branch of the lawn's showcase oak was truly artistic. My wife howled with horror, a sound more chilling than the scene out the window. I yelped (to lend more integrity to the production) and barked at absent servants to dial 911.

I was so happy with these results that I was contemplating a new trick that had to do with sperm whales when Mr. Hillerman's solution arrived. I sat down to an afternoon's reverie and contemplated the classical beauty of the mushroom. Mr. Hillerman's choice of weapon is so resonant and rich in allusion. Mushrooms are fairy tales. They are Jung's archetypal symbols. They are haute cuisine. They are sentinels of the corruption of nature. They are the poisons of kings. Mushrooms are history.

I threw myself into a study of mushrooms, quickly focusing my interest on the traits of the genus *Amanita*, always described in the books as "the most deadly poisonous." *Amanita*. What a lovely name! It seems to mean "little loved one."

The world of *Amanita* and its cousins, as you may know, is a many-splendored thing. The Jack-My-Lantern, orange as Halloween, long in the stalk and broad in the brim, is the perfect shade for a gnome. Its physical attractions are only surpassed by its deadliness. There is also Fly Agaric and Pungent Russula and the Death Angel. They are all beautiful compared to the gnarly grey phallic toadstools that nouvelle chefs pursue. And they are all fatal.

Most of the *Amanita* genus causes, as one tome put it,

"vomiting and diarrhea, pronounced flow of saliva, suppression of the urine, dizziness, derangement of vision and loss of confidence in ability to make ordinary movements, succeeded by drowsiness, stupor, cold sweating, and marked weakening of the heart's action." Two days of this life and then you die. Now, as an artist I am attracted to the possibilities here. I especially like the "pronounced flow of saliva." But, as I have said before, excess does not art make. So I pressed on to other sources.

I came across another rare species of *Amanita* that kills almost immediately, and contracts the muscles and skin of the face so quickly and violently that victims are often discovered with their nostrils splayed, their eyelids peeled back, and a demonic smile torn across the face from ear to ear. While this appeals on the level of the bizarre, it seems to me to be the effect one seeks in comic books or a late Friday night movie.

I pushed on in my work and eventually landed in the newspaper microfiche room of my local library. I wanted to know the latest in mushroom awareness. I came across an article about an extremely rare breed of *Amanita* that had been thought to be extinct. It had existed briefly in a particular basin of the Brazilian rain forest and then disappeared. Now, suddenly, it was showing up in abandoned coal mines or in shadowy alleys of ghost towns on the great plains. It's as if nature had brought back this deadliest of mushrooms to thrive in the most devastating wounds man had cut into the earth.

This mushroom is not as technicolorful as its kin. It has the gray and white appearance of a shiitake and is said, by those few unfortunates who might know, to taste "sort of like chicken." Its effect is to tighten the larynx enough to allow a slim column of air to rasp through, but not enough for intelligible speech. Minutes later, the joints begin to tighten, then stiffen and finally lock up. Victims typically pitch toward the ground with all the grace of a 4x8. There they flop about like fish, struggling toward an antidote that doesn't exist.

Spanish explorers in the New World discovered the ill effects of this particular breed during one of their frequent and fruitless mountain raids for gold. They had cooked the local mushrooms and immediately felt the effects. The bodies were found at varying distances from the cold ashes of the campfire contorted in alphabetical shapes. Two of the men, according to the bishop who chronicled this disaster in suspicious detail, were found "locked in the union that most sinfully profanes the name of God. Staring upon these frozen satyrs, I was reminded of the observation by a fellow monk that animals on the verge of sacrificial death smell the blood of their kind and, inexplicably, move to couple. Perhaps the Lord will forgive them." Naturally, as soon as I read these details, I knew I had discovered the perfect weapon.

But the next morning Ms. Caudwell's solution arrived in the mail, and I couldn't resist its possibilities. I was eager to imagine a solution that actually had me performing the act myself and so intimately. At the point of a knife, I was drawn to the concept that the method was as old as life—a knifing—but that the circumstances surrounding it had all the staging and melodrama of the *Ring Cycle*. This solution spanned several continents, had international implications, and made great use of costumes. Suddenly I was sampling different tartan patterns, setting the Campbell of Breadalbane against the Campbell of Argyll, the Mackenzie against the Mackintosh.

But then Mr. Block's letter arrived. How quickly I cast aside my kilt in order to gather a collection of body hair and to supplement that with nail parings and skin flakes. I explored the Lilliputian world of forensics. After slipping into Room 1507 once or twice (after a tryst; no one saw me enter), I had arrived to the point of amateur, able to distinguish between his and hers, and among the cranial, the pubic, and the eyebrow.

I had gathered enough small evidence to leave a forensic trail an inch wide, one any freshman gumshoe could follow and feel that he had come to his conclusions by his own Cartesian wits. Yet, as fate would have it, my wife announced that because of the continuing nightmares over the crab incident, she was carrying a can of Mace in her purse. She spoke of this to all her friends, setting up perfectly for Mr. Westlake's scenario. Once again, I was drawn to its charms. I had come full circle, so I sat down to think.

Each of the letters before me had any number of attractions. The sheer brazenness of Mr. Westlake, macing the lover and then handing him the gun so that he could stumble into an inexorable mesh of evidence. The theatricality of Mr. Lovesey, pranking myself to establish a maritime theme. And Mr. Hillerman, reinvigorating the historic classicity of the mushroom with the contemporaneity of the serial killing at the local grocery. The grand pomp of Ms. Caudwell, replete with fancy dress ball and the skirl of bagpipes. The postmodern drama of Mr. Block, played out on the stage of a microscope slide.

I set aside my nights of study and my days of action to consider my extraordinary dilemma. And it struck me that if murder can be an art, then those of us sitting in judgment must be practicing art criticism. So I put it to you. Were you in my place, which solution would you choose? Given that you might prefer your own, consider the company you keep and convince me to make the same choice. I am beginning to enjoy our correspondence.

FROM TONY HILLERMAN

PROSPECTIVE CLIENT:

*N*ow I learn that your original letter was not an assignment as you made it appear but a mere fishing expedition—an effort to pick my brains and those of four of my fellow practitioners without making a commitment to any of us. I consider such conduct reprehensible. I am sure the others you solicited feel the same. If your wife decides to turn the tables and do you in first, I would be happy to provide any guidance she might need.

But, though your behavior was at the sleazy level one expects only in Hollywood, your premise remains all too true. As you stated, murder as an art form is in a dreadful decline. The green pastures of crime in which the five of us graze have indeed turned dry and brown and need fertilization. The felony you propose offers that. Therefore, I will invest some more time to prevent you from screwing it up.

First, let me warn you away from Sarah Caudwell's advice. Indeed, Scotland offers some obvious advantages. Since Great Britain—and Scotland in particular—enjoy relatively little crime, the murder you propose would be noticed there.

119

Done properly, it would gain wide Scottish attention and probably even mention in the *Times* of London. But the tone of your letter indicates you wish more than that—and much more than that is needed. To leave America to compete for attention with a crime in the British Isles is like leaving Iceland to compete for the North Sahara kayak championship. Remember, a sequence of three or four similar homicides is enough to have Fleet Street proclaim a "serial killer." Bundy had done in about thirty in Florida and points West before anyone noticed, and he's still way down the list behind some Californians.

I concede that Sarah's proposal has élan. And the notion of having Blazes so thoroughly framed and frustrated has its appeal. But Sarah has overlooked the Peter Principle. What can go wrong *will* go wrong. Being a writer she should know all about what happens when one depends on tape recorders, and can imagine how the odds of disaster multiply when one adds the remote control element into the equation. None of us would be writers if we could master things more complicated than screwdrivers, doorknobs, and pencil sharpeners.

So take Ms. Caudwell's climactic scene and imagine what would really happen.

You allow the proper moments to tick away, anticipating the prerecorded scream.

Silence.

You wait a bit longer, sweat appearing on your brow.

Silence.

Then Blazes appears at the doorway, looking befuddled.

"I say," he says, "someone seems to have stabbed Tim's wife."

How do you handle that?

Or, worse:

You wait for the prerecorded scream.

A terrible sound emerges from the room, like the frantic quacking of a demented duck. You have done something or other wrong with the tape, as always seems to happen when writers try to use electronic devices intended for their betters, and it is running some forgotten conversation backward at rewind speed.

You rise to your feet, no longer having to pretend your intended panic, and shout: "My God, that's my wife—what the hell's happening to her?"

And another guest seated beside you will shout: "Ducks! Ducks in the house!"

Whereupon Blazes appears in the doorway, looking befuddled.

"I say," he says, "someone seems to have stabbed Tim's wife. And I think there are ducks in there. Under her dress."

In summation, I recommend you send Ms. Caudwell a polite note of dismissal. Forget Scotland. If you want an epic art-form murder, commit it in our native land, home of the National Rifle Association, where homicide kills more folks than the nineteen most common viruses, where violence is appreciated and understood. And above all, dismiss any notion of expecting electronic or mechanical devices to work for you. Why do you think the concierge of every hotel used on book-signing tours instructs bellhops to spend an extra five minutes showing visiting writers how the key works in the door, how to change channels on the TV set, how to avoid scalding in the shower, how to manage the telephone?

And while you are writing the note for Caudwell, run

off a second copy for Peter Lovesey. No American would cite George Joseph Smith, whose bag total was only three, as a serial killer. The English have no sense of proportion in such matters.

Admittedly Lovesey's scheme would get a better press than Mistress Caudwell's. Alas, however, once again the Peter Principle applies.

Lovesey sets up his clever deception with a series of self-imposed practical jokes—climaxing with one grotesque and expensive enough to attract the press. Or, if not the press, at least the TV cameras. This is indeed astute and upon it depends, if not the success of the homicide, at least the certainty that it will become a homicide celebrated enough to meet your requirements for posthumous fame. (Alas, once we would have called this notoriety.) But what actually happens?

About the time the inflated whale is secured atop the house and the interior converted into an aquarium something more important will certainly happen somewhere. "Kill that story about the breakthrough on cheap fission power and those items about the cancer cure and the Nazi coup toppling Chancellor Kohl," news editors will be shouting, "the Queen's second cousin has developed hangnails. And to make room for pictures, kill that inflated whale piece." And at BBC-TV, the image of you looking gravely into the lens with a background of tropical fish is being erased from videotapes to make room for one hundred and eighteen seconds of a physician explaining that while royal hangnails are rarely fatal they are inevitably inconvenient. If you are carrying this off in America substitute Donald Trump or some other member of our version of royalty. It doesn't matter. Something will crowd your practical joke out of TV time and all will be more or less for naught.

Your wife, you say, would still be dead. Maybe, but you won't have raised murder to the Sistine Chapel ceiling. Without the well-publicized sequence of jokes, this business of killing somebody with a squid, or whatever that beast is that Lovesey is selling you, wouldn't make it as a historic crime. Exotic, true, but hardly memorable. I'll wager you can't remember who committed the snake-in-the-mailbox caper of a few years ago, or even the identity of the two kidnappers who buried a school bus full of students in California a bit earlier. No. To make death by Jellyfish in the Jacuzzi memorable in this sated world, Lovesey wisely saw you have to set up a sequence.

But there are other flaws as well. They're not failures of Lovesey's imagination, but products of his European background. Lovesey presumes a level of efficiency, or things happening when and how they are supposed to happen, which is totally foreign to this side of the Atlantic. I will cite a single example.

In setting up your crime while protecting your alibi, Lovesey instructs you as follows:

"You take the 3 P.M. [flight], which gets you back to your hometown by 3:45." Thereupon he allows you two hours and fifteen minutes to walk to Boylan's garage, don your laboratory costume, drive to the laboratory, steal the jellyfish, plant incriminating clues, get home no earlier than 5:10 to make sure that the maid will have departed (the Peter Principle provides, of course, that on this day she *won't* have departed; she will be taking advantage of your absence to entertain friends in your living room), deposit the jellyfish in the 80-degree Jacuzzi (if your thermostat is as temperamental as mine, that jellyfish will become either stewed or chilled to total lethargy), hustle back to the Boylan homestead, leave car and assorted clues, and fly back to your fishing spa. "There is one [flight] at 6 P.M.," Lovesey assures you. And indeed, it all seems to click together as smoothly as a British railroad timetable.

Alas, alas. Therein lies the problem. Lovesey's confidence is based on habitual use of British public transportation, where planes, trains, and even buses leave and arrive as scheduled. You and I, veterans of American public transportation, know better. Even as I write this, the U.S. Open Tennis competition is being held at Flushing Meadow, which I gather is near New York's La Guardia airport. The fatuous fellow announcing this event for the TV network has just told his straight man in the broadcasting booth that the audience and players won't be annoyed this year by the sound of passing airliners. It seems the mayor, himself a tennis fan, arranged for flights to be rerouted. I mention this not to illustrate to Peter and Sarah that we, despite our democratic pretensions, have a privileged class but to note that if your flights to establishing your alibi happened to be through La Guardia on that day you would have been squirming in one of those miserable plastic airport chairs with tens of thousands of common folks—your plans gone awry because the establishment wished to avoid irritating the spoiled darlings cursing and snarling at the referees on the courts or the social elite watching them.

Of course you could schedule the murder to avoid such events. But be realistic. The 3 P.M. printed in the airline timetable means only that the plane won't leave *before* that time. When it will leave, only God knows. I formed several lasting friendships waiting in the airport at Boise, Idaho, because the pilot decided not to board us until he could get permission to land at Denver's notoriously overtaxed airport. I read enough of *Foucault's Pendulum* to reach almost catatonic boredom while waiting for my plane to leave the Chicago airport.

Your flight "gets you back to your hometown by 3:45," Lovesey says. Forget it. With a little luck you enter the holding pattern about 4:10, touch down about 5:05, get clearance to connect to the gate about 14 minutes later, and actually stumble into the terminal at 5:32. By the time you get downstairs to discover your luggage didn't make it, it's time to rush back upstairs to catch that 6 P.M. flight back to the fishing lodge.

But don't bother to rush, because the video screen will show that it's 30 minutes late.

Well, then, how about Lawrence Block? His plots are as astute as Lovesey's or Caudwell's, and—being American—he is familiar with our native problems. The solution he offers you is certainly clever and seems to meet all of your criteria.

Seems to meet. Be warned, prospective client. Reread Lawrence Block. Notice the subtlety of his plots. In the distinguished company of mystery writers, Lawrence Block is known as an intellectual; as a man who does not suffer fools gladly. As the tone of his letter makes clear, he considers you a foolish man. He holds you in contempt. He is playing a game with you. He is setting you up for disaster.

The scheme Mr. Block gives you, involving a sequence of murders with trademark characteristics and its climax leaving Blazes Boylan deliciously framed, has distinct appeal. Even though you report that your wife now carries a Mace dispenser in her purse, I fear you will be tempted back to it. (You might, for example, slip the can from her purse in her absence, exhaust its contents Macing resident cockroaches, and return the empty can.)

Avoid that temptation. Here's why.

Yesterday's *Albuquerque Journal* carried a report of a disagreement in Philadelphia. Over a period of eight months, eight young women have disappeared from various Philadelphia bars, only later to turn up dead. The local press has concluded from this the possibility of a serial killer. But the local cops declare themselves skeptical. Since such events (contrary to the impression Block would give you) are routine, it might as well be eight different murderers as a hardworking single.

Why am I telling you this? Because this isn't England, where murder is rare, treasured, and worthy of close scrutiny. Even if you don't stop at 5, even if you run the score up to 8, or 18, or 80, how can you count on the police to notice if (statistically speaking) nothing unusual is happening? And the more you do it, the more you increase the risk that one of these bimbos you pick up has intentions as murderous as your own and will be armed with something worse than Mace.

I concede that Dame Agatha Christie used this idea with great success in her *The ABC Murders* and the book has become a classic. But that was set in England, a gentler place, and the year was 1936—gentler times. When Ed McBain revived the idea for one of his police procedurals a generation later he had to modify the plot considerably to make it work in America.

In summation: Forget Block.

Which brings us to the distinguished Donald Westlake

and his proposal that you establish a double identity and thus serve as your own alibi. Very clever and so simple that it might work were it not, alas, for the Peter Principle again— and the business of the hotel key.

First, there's the matter of getting Blazes Boylan to fire a pistol on the gun club range. As you describe him Boylan seems the sort who would flinch away from guns, and while it may be true, as Westlake states, that "Psychologically, he cannot refuse" membership after you set him up for it, he can, psychologically, stall off the day when he actually has to fire a pistol. Such stalling and foot-dragging are normally only an irritation, but when the timing of a murder depends on getting that burned powder into the skin of Boylan's fingers, I predict it will become a major problem.

"Can't manage it today, old fellow. Handball with Roger."

"Sorry. Bit of a headache this morning. The noise would make it worse."

You'll hear those and a thousand other excuses until one day you'll find yourself deciding that Boylan must be the victim instead of your wife.

But let's say you actually get him to fire the damned pistol. Says Westlake: ". . . the criminological laboratory's tests *will* [the italics are Westlake's] demonstrate that Blazes has recently fired a gun." Will they? I have just read a news account in which a woman is suing a laboratory for getting the blood type (a much simpler, more foolproof test) of every single member of her family wrong.

Perhaps, even probably, the test will show up the burned powder. We'll say nothing went wrong on this day. The lab tech was unusually sober, his cigar ashes didn't dribble into the solution rendering the results "inconclusive." He didn't pull the wrong bottle of chemicals out of the locker. The Peter Principle took a vacation. *Probably* everything will work as planned. But remember, your life will depend on it.

And this element of chance isn't the worst of it. Once you get those powder burns into Boylan's skin, you are committed to a tight schedule. Every passing moment produces a bit of body oil, a bit of sweat, a bit of friction, which reduces the powder, and the chances of its detection, a trifle. Every shower and hand washing reduces it much more. Once Boylan quits stalling and shoots the pistol, you are in a hurry. That's dangerous.

Which brings us to the hotel and to Room 1507.

Mr. Westlake's fame among mystery readers is long established. For him the day has passed when his publisher's marketing people bundle him up and send him off on those awful tests of stamina known as book tours. Thus, while Westlake remembers that a hotel with a room number as high as 1507 must be a big hotel, he seems not to know what has happened to hotel keys in such monstrous places. We who still must endure these mind-numbing journeys from one hotel to another know that Room 1507 isn't opened by a key these days. The hotel key is another victim of America's progress in crime and technology. The door to Room 1507 these days is opened by a little rectangular strip of stiff plastic. The hotel patron slips this into a slot on the door. When he finally manages to insert it proper side up and proper side out and to the proper depth with the proper authority, it causes something to click and unlocks the door. Thus there is no passkey to press into Silly Putty for subsequent reproduction. Nor is there any use in saving the little plastic strip for future use after you have checked into Room 1507 to reconnoiter it. In their continuing efforts to stay a jump ahead of criminals (such as yourself and Westlake) the hotels change the magnetic coding in these locks so that the strip which opens 1507 on Tuesday will open 1384 on Wednesday—thereby baffling the burglars.

You can probably rely enough on our airlines to carry out Westlake's alibi plan, since no close timing is involved. (I say probably, because of personal memories: a dismal night spent in a Dallas Holiday Inn, courtesy of Delta Airlines, when I was supposed to be cozy in my own bunk in Albuquerque; trying to explain to a Denver bookstore seven minutes before a book signing was supposed to start there how I could be calling from the Salt Lake City airport, etc.) The alibi plan itself is sheer genius. I wish I had thought of it and I fully intend to plagiarize it as soon as enough time passes to make the theft seem less obvious. But you won't need the alibi if you can't get into the room to do the dastardly deed.

I have one final quibble. As Westlake instructs you, you shoot your wife twice, cause Boylan to grovel, then seem to come to your senses when he asks for the gun.

I quote Westlake: "You hand it to him, spray him with Mace, drop the can near your wife's body . . . and leave." (Disguised as a little old lady in a motorized wheelchair, as I recall the Westlakean scenario.) All very well, but I write this with a razor scrape burning on my chin, the scrape being caused by the failure of my Burma Shave spray can (which uses a mechanism very similar to Westlake's Mace sprayer) to deliver shaving cream when I pushed its button this morning. Thus the scenario in Room 1507 deteriorates into something like this:

"You hand him the gun, push the button on the Mace can, and, when nothing sprays forth, shake it desperately. Boylan shoots you in the gizzard with your pistol. You drop the Mace can near your wife's body and leave on a stretcher, disguised as a murder suspect heading off to prison."

My penultimate advice: Eschew depending on Mace until you can find a roll-on dispenser. And always, always remember: What can go wrong will go wrong.

My ultimate advice: First, adopt my scheme fully and completely. Do not pamper yourself by avoiding that unpleasant first step of telling the fuzz that you drowned your wife. It is essential to get the cops in the properly adversarial mood. Second, take very seriously the enclosed sheet listing my charges and send the required poundage of used $20 bills via United Parcel Service, Federal Express, or some other private delivery system which will not involve the U.S. Postal Service. It has become as unreliable as Mace dispensers, airlines, and laboratory tests, and there's no reason to involve the federal authorities in our business affairs.

I recommend prompt—indeed instant—payment of my bill. What's the hurry? As I read that first letter of yours soliciting my help in this felonious effort, I noticed the paper seemed a bit more fragile than one would expect. It was brittle. Faintly and unevenly discolored. Prematurely aged. Something was amiss. I rushed it to my Xerox machine (which happened to be working) and made several clear copies, taking care that the final page and your signature were perfectly legible. I did the same with your equally incriminating second letter. Now, almost as you had planned, both of the original letters have crumbled away in my filing cabinet to something resembling ash. But I have plenty of copies for the police, if you carry out the plan but neglect to pay, or for your wife if your nerve fails you.

It was a clever idea, treating those letters with acid. But for once, the postman was prompt.

What could go wrong did go wrong.

FROM PETER LOVESEY

Sir,

*Y*our letter astonished me. Your wife is still breathing.

I am at a loss to understand why.

I expected my payment, the check for a million dollars. To say that I am disappointed is an understatement. I am enraged. I am foaming at the mouth. I handed you a masterpiece—the Jellyfish in the Jacuzzi—and what have you done with it? Recognized it for the beautiful thing it is and secured its place of honor in the Pantheon of Crime? No, you have left it to gather dust, neglected, disregarded. Worse, you have betrayed my genius. You have passed on my perfect plot to a bunch of mystery writers.

I hear that Lawrence Block's next book is to be entitled *The Burglar Who Pilfered Jellyfish*. Donald E. Westlake is at this moment tapping out the last paragraph of *Dortmunder and the Big Sting*. Sarah Caudwell (a slower writer) is trying to devise a first sentence involving a whirlpool and the law. And Tony Hillerman claims to have been told by a medicine man that Navajo sand paintings are based on a jellyfish

133

motif—which, of course, will decorate the jacket of his forth-coming book, *Hidden Stings*.

Each of them will be hearing from my lawyers.

As for you, sir, I would cheerfully dump you in your Jacuzzi and sling in one of your giant crabs. You don't *deserve* my brilliant help. You actually embarked on my plan. As I suggested, you obtained the duplicates of Boylan's keys. Nice work. And there was more. By good fortune, you are a fisherman (I should have divined it from your self-glorifying) and you took the necessary steps to publicize your devotion to the sport. Clearly, you took up the piscatorial joking with relish. The crabs were a happy embellishment of my idea. I'm willing to bet you got some media coverage. The plot was in top gear, racing to its destination.

Then you dropped it, diverted by Mr. Hillerman's mushrooms. *Mushrooms.* I ask you! Where's the alliteration? *Murder with Mushrooms?* How commonplace. Forty years ago, the man who founded the Crime Writers' Association, of which I am currently chairman, the late John Creasey, wrote a novel with precisely that title, but Creasey was the first to admit that he didn't have time to lavish on brilliant titles; he published over 500. As I thought I explained in my first letter, if you truly aspire to immortality, your method of murder must be reducible to some vivid, unforgettable phrase. *The Brides in the Bath,* or, with a neat, postmodern refinement, *The Jellyfish in the Jacuzzi.*

You express some partiality for the word *Amanita.* True, the term has a certain rarefied charm, but it will never gain common currency, never bring you the posthumous fame that Mr. Hillerman promises. Beware of Tony Hillerman. He's too kindhearted. He hasn't told you the truth—that you're a megalomaniac, in my phrase; a patina'd underachiever, in Mr. Westlake's; and an ineffectual toy husband, in Mr. Block's. And if Tony hasn't been frank about your personality defects, how can you trust his recipe for murder?

It is, after all, a tasteless dish, almost as revolting as Mr. Block's, of which more anon. It involves the murder of at least eighteen hapless gourmet customers of the Yummie Yuppie Deli. This number, Mr. Hillerman blithely suggests, could be higher. Isn't that what you Americans succinctly describe as overkill? We mystery writers were commissioned to suggest a way of killing your wife, not most of your neighbors as well. I do object to slaughter on this scale; some of the victims could be buyers of my books.

However, I bow to the brilliance of Mr. Hillerman's concept of bluffing the investigators by admitting to murder. It's a delightful twist. If he had devised a way of poisoning your wife without poisoning half of America at the same time, I would be willing to give it a grudging nod. The problem is that the police will be interested to know how everyone else died—how the poisonous mushrooms got into the display at the Yummie Yuppie Deli. They do have seventeen other homicides to account for. I would expect them to question every customer and store assistant that day, seeking descriptions of everyone who passed through the shop. Even if you were not spotted adding the poisonous fungi to the display, you must have been seen making the other purchases, to acquire the sales slip that you later smuggled into Blazes's pocket. It's a local shop. You're known there.

You've blown it.

Forget it.

Since I mentioned Mr. Lawrence Block's prescription, I'd better dispose of it. I find his method almost as profligate as Tony Hillerman's, and much more messy. All those women, innocent except for a willingness to go to bed with you, murdered and mutilated? It's overkill with trimmings, if you'll excuse the double entendre. Four killings, he suggests, to establish Blazes as a serial murderer. That may not be random slaughter on the Hillerman scale, but it's still expensive in human lives (four more bookstore customers, I keep thinking). And the ghoulish collecting of souvenirs demands the callousness of a true psychopath. I don't really think of you as a psychopath, though I may have tossed in the word in passing.

Let's be generous. The Lawrence Block method has a Grand Guignol quality that might just get you a footnote in the history of crime. It has the blood and guts; what it lacks is the poetry. Without wishing to labor my theme, how can it be encapsulated in a few unforgettable words? Why are Jack the Ripper's crimes remembered a century later? Not because of the ripping, as Mr. Block would have you believe. No, it's the brilliance of the name. Jack the Ripper. Inspired. We are told by those who make a study of Jack's horrible killings—Ripperologists, they term themselves—that three letters, and only three, of the thousands sent to the police and press in 1888 are thought to have been penned by the murderer. They contain knowledge of the crimes that no one else could have acquired. The one sent on 25 September, 1888, was the first to use the title Jack the Ripper. Before that, the killer was known to the press as Leather Apron. How banal! A second Jack the Ripper letter was posted on 30 September. The third, enclosing a section of kidney from the latest victim, was unsigned, but gave the murderer's address as "From Hell." Brilliant! Jack the Ripper was a pure-born crime writer, no question. If someone had awarded him a Gold Dagger or an Edgar after he sent this first letter, the other victims would have been spared.

So you'd better think of a pithy, evocative name if you want to be remembered as a serial killer. There are too many in the trade these days. The Boston Strangler. The Yorkshire Ripper. The Zodiac Killer. They try their best.

On a more practical point, I have the gravest doubts whether you or anyone could commit four murders and decapitations without leaving some trace of yourself that would conflict with the planted evidence. Forensic teams are pretty good at picking up disregarded hairs and fragments of skin tissue. And DNA analysis is improving all the time.

I don't see you as a latter-day Ripper.

Sorry.

Let's turn to Miss Caudwell's Caledonian extravaganza. It has plenty to commend it: the tartans, the jewels, the flattering glow of candlelight, and the icy glitter of the skene-dhu. Here, I thought, when I started Sarah's letter, is a winning formula. We Brits have a precious asset: our history is irresistible to you Americans. By staging the murder in Scotland, she not only gives it a sense of occasion, she helps the British tourist industry. Edinburgh during the festival. The castle atop its granite outcrop; Princes Street; the Scott Memorial; Holyrood Palace. What a setting!

Before you book the flights, take a second look at the scenario. Is it to be played out on the castle battlements to the mournful skirl of a lone piper? Or in the Palace of Holyrood, where Mary, Queen of Scots, resided, and where her unfortunate secretary, Rizzio, was dragged from her presence and dispatched with fifty-seven dagger thrusts? Is it to be staged on the doorstep of 11 Picardy Place, where Sir Arthur Conan Doyle was born?

No, it takes place in a hotel room.

Oh, what anticlimax! At bottom, stripped of its tartan accessories, the scene of the murder selected by Miss Caudwell is as dreary as Mr. Block's or Mr. Westlake's—a room with a number, and adjacent bathroom, and electric kettle, and an abstract print on the wall. You've flown three thousand miles to Room 1507 in the Edinburgh Holiday Inn.

Moreover, it's messy. Not so messy as Mr. Block's series of murders, but bloody nevertheless. A stabbing isn't clean, like a jellyfish in a Jacuzzi. Some immediate laundering of your shirt cuffs may be necessary, Miss Caudwell cautions. She has kitted you in full Scottish costume, with plaid cloak, jacket, white shirt, cravat, sporran, kilt, socks, and shoes. You're unaccustomed to it. Dressed as you are, like Bonnie Prince Charlie, can you carry out a clean stabbing, move the body to the bed, secrete the tape recorder in the folds of her dress, without getting blood on your clothes? And then in the short time before suspicion is aroused by the length of your absence, can you wash off any stains with cold water, examine yourself in the mirror, return to your guests, and mingle unconcernedly? With your plaid cloak tight around you to cover the stains, you're going to cut a faintly ridiculous figure in a centrally heated hotel.

Thumbs down, reluctantly, to the Scottish play.

Which leaves you with the Westlake solution, or mine. Donald E. Westlake has devised a plot that I am bound to admit is brilliant. I am bound to admit it because to an amazing degree Mr. Westlake's method overlaps my own. If I didn't know for a fact that he types his deathless prose on a thirty-year-old Smith Corona portable, I'd believe that Westlake had hacked his way into my computer. Just examine the evidence.

From Peter Lovesey

Having delivered his masterly analysis of your personality defects, and, with total conviction, named Blazes Boylan as your real intended victim, Mr. Westlake outlines his plot:

1. You take up an outdoor sport and encourage Blazes to join you. In Westlake's scenario, it is shooting; in mine, fishing.

2. You contrive to obtain an imprint of the key to Room 1507 at the inn. Westlake has Plans A, B and C; mine is another variant, but the object is the same.

3. To establish your alibi on the day of the killing, you take a flight to another locality, and then make a secret, unscheduled flight back, returning secretly after the murder. The plots are identical in this strategem.

Remarkable, isn't it? Was it a case of great minds thinking alike? Or does Don Westlake have a spy working for him? Or am I becoming paranoid?

The rest of his plot is a letdown. I mean, it will probably work—the stuff in Room 1507 with the gun in the gloved hand and the Mace—but where's the Art that makes it the perfect masterpiece? The ornamentation, the proper sense of the grotesque that is the hallmark of the baroque? As you, sir, remarked in the brief you gave us, perfect murders are easy. What you required of us was "not the perfect murder, but the perfect masterpiece . . . a crime so beautiful in construction and so ingenious in practice that it aspires to the condition of art . . . baroque in concept and rich in detail."

It's another squalid killing in a hotel room.

God knows, I've tried to be generous to my fellow

139

professionals, picking out the finer points in their scenarios, but I can't in all conscience recommend you to follow their advice. Two of the plots, in my opinion, are colorful, but dangerous; you won't get away with them. The other two are intriguing in buildup, but disappointing in execution.

Review it now. Consider the weapons we propose. Tony Hillerman's toxic mushrooms, Larry Block's knife, Sarah Caudwell's skene-dhu, and Don Westlake's gun. Then consider *Chironex fleckeri,* my poisonous jellyfish. Is there any contest?

Compare the buildup to each killing. The visit to Dr. Dottage, the swift work in the deli, and *The ABC Murders* open on Boylan's pillow. The decapitations and the distributing of pubic hairs. The trip to Scotland, the partygoing, and the substitution of the daggers. The resurrection of Minor DeMortis, the shooting lessons, and the casing of Room 1507.

Now consider the buildup I gave you: the shark at the front door, the house filled with fishtanks, the whale on the roof, and the Chocolate Binge. These are concepts that elevate murder into a new postmodern era. We're into surrealism here. Can you imagine any cop capable of understanding it?

The last, crucial element is the killing. I devised a means of dispatch that is bizarre, unique, baroque, but safe. You'll be 150 miles away when the lady dies. No need to drag the poisoned body to the bathroom; or slice bits off before Blazes arrives on the scene; or do a Lady Macbeth washing the spots from your hands; or shoot one of the lovers and spray the other. The jellyfish takes care of it. And the shock value of the killing is so much better.

I have almost finished. My analysis is complete. The case

for the sea wasp is overwhelming. But I have to state that I trust you not at all. Your second letter confirms you as a ditherer, infirm of purpose. I have a stomach-churning suspicion that you'll try to work out some shallow compromise from all the conflicting advice we have delivered.

Don't.

I am tormented by a vision. You are dressed in Scottish costume—having acquired a false identity as the drunken Nobel Prize–winner, Weldon McWeinie—your sporran stuffed with pubic hairs and mushrooms, a can of Mace in one hand, an automatic in the other, and you are circling confusedly around the rim of your Jacuzzi, in which are ugly little bits of the bodies of your reviled wife and Blazes Boylan and Georgia and Ben and a couple of detectives and the famous giant crabs of Japan.

Stand firm. No compromise. It's all or nothing, and it has to be the Jellyfish in the Jacuzzi. To quote Lady Macbeth once more, screw your courage to the sticking-place, and we'll not fail. And kindly mail me my check by return.

FROM SARAH CAUDWELL

My Dear Tim,

I begin to have misgivings. I open my newspaper with increasing apprehension. Any day now I shall read of a series of women who have been found in their baths apparently stung to death by jellyfish, but discovered, upon closer examination, to have succumbed to mushroom poisoning. Soon after that it will be reported that another such incident has occurred in Edinburgh, at a time when the husband of the victim claims to have been in the company of a mysterious woman named Diana.

No, Tim, this really will not do. You are, I appreciate, a novice in the art of murder, and display both the virtues and the failings of that condition: If one is touched by your enthusiasm, one should not reflect too harshly on the undiscernment which is, I suppose, its inevitable concomitant. Let me remind you again, however, that you have expressed the ambition to be not merely a murderer but an artist. If you are to succeed, you must resist the temptation to cram willy-nilly into your intended masterpiece everything which momentarily catches your fancy, without reflecting on its

143

relationship with the other elements in your work and its place in the overall scheme.

You must learn to select—not only to reject bad ideas, but also to discard good ideas if they do not assist your final purpose. The Parthenon and St. Paul's Cathedral are both very beautiful buildings, but putting the dome of St. Paul's on top of the Parthenon would not produce a still more beautiful one. You must learn, above all, not to overdo things.

My distinguished colleagues, in their answers to your first communication, have already been somewhat severe in their censure, and are unlikely, I fear, to be less so in replying to your second. I am reluctant to distress you by adding to their reproaches—like you, I dislike causing pain; but my conscience does not permit me to say that they are unjustified.

It is Mr. Westlake, I dare say, who will feel that he has the most cause to be vexed with you. He will point out, I imagine, that he has devised for you, at considerable personal sacrifice—he might have used it for his own next novel—a plan of great beauty and artistic elegance, and that you, by your rash and self-indulgent action, have rendered it entirely useless. Against this accusation it is impossible to defend you.

Let us consider, in case you have failed to appreciate it, wherein lies the artistic beauty of Mr. Westlake's plan. We begin with a simple, commonplace problem: a man is about to commit a murder and requires a witness to provide him with an alibi. One solution would be for him to bribe a complete outsider—someone not in any other way involved in the situation giving rise to the murder—to give false evidence on his behalf. This solution, as you will see, has little or no artistic merit: a truthful or apparently truthful account of it would have, at best, the interest of a good piece of jounalism.

One of the most serious defects is that it offends the artistic principle of economy: the introduction of a character for the sole purpose of supplying an alibi, with no other part to play in the story, is wasteful and slovenly, and thus repugnant to Art. We might try to remedy this by making the witness someone who has some further role in the drama— the woman, let us say, not straining to avoid the obvious, on whose account our hero wishes to rid himself of his wife. Well, that is better from the point of view of economy; but the eventual disclosure that the lady is lying is hardly calculated, in such circumstances, to produce a thrill of astonishment.

We still lack, in short, a peripeteia—that complete reversal of the situation which Aristotle tells us is essential to a truly dramatic plot structure. We might therefore further modify our solution by concealing the relationship between the witness and our hero and making her someone who would be expected to be indifferent or hostile to him—let us say, for example, his inspector of taxes. We begin now to have the makings of an artistically satisfying plot.

Consider, however, the superiority of Mr. Westlake's proposal to even this much improved situation. It provides the alibi without making addition to the minimum cast of characters necessary for a murder—the murderer and the victim: it is the very quintessence of economy. Moreover, it deceives the audience (that is to say the outside observer) not merely as to the motives and attributes of a character in the drama but as to the character's very existence: the way is thus prepared for a magnificent peripeteia when the truth is finally revealed.

And what have you done? Despite Mr. Westlake's careful and detailed advice, and for no better reason, so far as I can see, than that you thought it would be amusing, you have created an alter ego who is a woman. Have you still not realized that this is fatal to any chance of success?

Yes, fatal.

The artistic brilliance of Mr. Westlake's plan should not blind us to the fact that from the practical point of view it is—how shall I put it?—just a trifle on the chancy side. There is Blazes Boylan, sitting in his cell, knowing that he saw you commit murder and that therefore your alibi must be false, and presumably saying so, vociferously and often, to the police, his lawyers, and the press. If, despite this, none of them feels that the alibi witness should be questioned a little more closely, it can only be because he seems to be a person with no imaginable motive for telling lies on your behalf. Do you really think, in that context, that a boring middle-aged businessman can safely be replaced by an attractive young woman in $500 shoes?

If you survive unscathed the indignation of Mr. West-lake, I can see little hope of your escaping the wrath of Mr. Lovesey. Indeed, unless he happens to find in his thesaurus some even more irresistible term of abuse than *slubberdegullion*, I seriously question whether Mr. Lovesey will bring himself to reply at all to your most recent letter. If he does, I suspect that it will be only in the hope of securing payment of the large sums of money which he apparently expects to receive from you.

I am referring, I need hardly to say, to the incident of the giant crabs.

To begin with the least important, that is to say the practical aspect of the matter: What steps have you taken to ensure that responsibility for the crabs will ultimately be attributed to Blazes Boylan? None, so far as I can see, though

Mr. Lovesey made it clear in his letter that the inculpation of Boylan was a vital element of all the practical jokes in the apparent campaign against you.

Even taking the optimistic view—namely that you are right in believing your "fixer" to be genuinely unaware of your identity—this episode has achieved nothing more useful than a brief frisson of somewhat meretricious excitement. I myself am unable to take the optimistic view: a man of that calling does not omit the elementary precaution of finding out the names and addresses of his customers, and if they prove to be involved in any serious criminal activity he sings, as the expression is, like a canary.

Such willful and wanton incompetence is almost beyond belief—I am half tempted to hope that you have omitted something in your account of this transaction. But alas—I know you now too well to think it likely that you have been reticent about your achievements. Those of my colleagues who are versed in psychology may perhaps suggest that there is some deeper explanation than mere carelessness: such a pride in your exploit that your subconscious could not endure the thought of its being attributed to Boylan. This, if they are right, portends ill for your larger enterprise.

I do not wish to duplicate what Mr. Lovesey may already have said to you, doubtless in more bitter and eloquent terms. I must point out, however, since his habitual modesty will perhaps prevent him from doing so, that quite apart from its practical consequences your escapade has entirely wrecked the fine artistic structure of the plan which he devised for you. The central feature of his original conception was a series of incidents developing in a graceful progression from the mischievous to the homicidal—an effect, please understand, not to be achieved by mere accident, or without the exercise of care and judgment. What place is there, in this charming and elegant sequence, for your outsized crustaceans?

In my opinion, none—though, since you had evidently set your heart on them, one might have agreed to their being inserted between the dead shark and the plastic whale. It would not have been right, but it would have been no worse a concession than other artists have made to the taste of their patrons. As an initial incident, however, they are completely inadmissible. It is clear—or should be so to anyone with the slightest sense of proportion or climax—that the scene with the shark, not only delightful in itself but also an indispensable signal to the theme and motive of the sequence as a whole, must come at the beginning. To put it after the scene with the crabs reduces it to anticlimax, and the entire design is ruined. As I have said, I do not want to be harsh—but this is sheer vandalism.

At least you seem to have done nothing as yet to compromise the admirable plan proposed by Mr. Hillerman. I am assuming, of course—in view of the rest of your performance, I may be being unduly optimistic—that your newfound learning on the subject of mushrooms was not acquired by simply waltzing into your local library and borrowing, wholesale and in your own name, every volume on poisonous fungi to be found on the shelves.

With your usual rapid grasp of the inessentials, you regard the mushrooms as the most important element of Mr. Hillerman's plan. In fact they are a merely incidental feature, though admittedly an attractive one. For once I am able to agree with you—the historical and mystical associations are extremely pleasing. You will find particular pleasure, no doubt, in remembering that they were used for a similar purpose by the Emperor Nero—a young man, as you will recall, who also enjoyed dressing up in women's clothes and was always anxious for recognition of his talents as an artist. (Though it was his mother, Agrippina, if my memory serves me, whom he dispatched by this particular method—his wife he disposed of by less sophisticated means.)

The essential feature of Mr. Hillerman's plan, however, is the creation of a structure which reveals you at the outset as the murderer, then conclusively shows that you are not the murderer, and finally reveals, to the astonishment of the audience, that you are the murderer after all. (By "your audience" I mean, if all goes well, the readers of your post-humously published memoirs; if ill, of course, the police.) This is a structure of dazzling audacity and brilliance, and if you can bring it off it will be without question a very considerable artistic achievement.

And yet, while I am reluctant to discourage you from an enterprise of such artistic quality, it is perhaps my duty to repeat at this point my earlier warning to you—that between Life and Art there are certain significant differences. One of these is that in a play or a novel the dramatis personae can generally be relied on to behave in character—their existence depends on it. In life it is otherwise.

Mr. Hillerman's plan relies on a skillful and ingenious use of character—the propensity of policemen to disbelieve what they are told—to bring about the natural and convincing development of events toward the intended climax. From the artistic point of view, this is admirable; but suppose that in real life the investigating officer does not behave in character?

Suppose that he is idle, or incompetent, or in love with his wife and anxious to get home, and has no desire to ques-

tion the obvious explanation? Suppose that the rather in-
experienced doctor who conducts the autopsy—the more
senior ones being fully occupied with the mushroom poi-
sonings—does not notice, or is embarrassed to point out, the
inconsistencies between your account and the medical evidence? Suppose that the time for your trial draws closer, and
your lawyer is negotiating with the prosecution for a reduc-
tion in your sentence (say from twenty-five years to twenty)
to reflect your candor and remorse for your crime, and still
no one has raised the possibility that your confession should
not be taken at face value—what will Mr. Hillerman advise
you to do then? When, of course, the one thing you certainly
cannot do is suggest to anyone that the evidence should be
reexamined.

Should you decide, having reflected on this possibility,
that the high artistic rewards he offers you are nonetheless not quite worth that particular risk, I shall not take
it on myself to blame you. The choice you are left with, in
that case, will be between Mr. Block's solution and my own.

Mr. Block's solution I would rule out on artistic
grounds—that is to say, as being both morally and aesthet-
ically repulsive. I need make, I think, no apology to Mr. Block
for saying so, since he himself has been at pains to tell you
that murder is not and cannot be artistic, being of its very
nature an act of monstrous brutality. Perhaps implicitly re-
buking those of us who would allow you to believe otherwise,
who let you imagine murder as an affair of elegance and
artifice, of rubies and champagne, he has offered you a solution designed to demonstrate that murder is a sordid and
disgusting business—not at all the thing to be chattered about
over cocktails, still less read about during lunch.

His purpose, it would seem at first sight, is to concentrate your mind on the grim realities of murder, and thus to discourage you from committing it: if so, then plainly his position is morally impeccable. And yet, if that is indeed his purpose, how curiously he goes about it. He begins by suggesting that you do not mean what you say—that you really have no serious intention of harming either your wife or your friend. This conclusion, however, does not give him the satisfaction one might expect—he does not congratulate you on being a better man than you have led us to suppose. On the contrary, he contemptuously derides you for being indecisive and ineffectual—for being, he seems to be saying, not man enough to kill anyone.

One somehow begins, despite the urbanity of Mr. Block's literary style, to hear echoes of the school playground—of one small boy daring another, with taunts of "sissy" and "Mummy's boy," to pull some little girl's pigtails or tie a can to the tail of the school cat. And as he guides you down the unpleasant paths of butchery and mutilation, pointing out their horrors with the zeal of a puritan conscientiously measuring every inch of flesh on display in the strip club, his tone still somehow seems always to imply that to contemplate them without flinching will be a proof of your manhood and a passport to his regard.

Your other advisors, it is true, have done little to draw your attention to the nastier aspects of murder: you may even perhaps have begun to suspect that we are really not very much interested in killing people, but rather in the art of ingenious deception. Have we, by our omission of the disagreeable details, encouraged you to believe that murder is a seemly and acceptable pastime?

I should not like to think so, nor indeed do I. I draw comfort from the reflection that in England in the 1920s and

151

'30s, when the genteel murder mystery was at the height of
its popularity, there appears to have been no corresponding
increase in the level of homicide. Members of the peerage
were able to spend quite long periods in their libraries without being stabbed by any of their relatives; a number of tea
parties took place at which the vicar refrained from putting
arsenic in the cucumber sandwiches; and remarkably few of
the butlers employed in country houses considered it proper
to enliven the weekend by shooting one or two of the guests.

It is possible, I suppose, that Mr. Block's solution to your
problem will appeal to you more than the others which have
been proposed. It may be that your wish to murder your
wife has nothing to do with her individual qualities or with
the specific difficulties of your relationship—that what you
really want is to kill not a particular woman, but any woman,
indeed if it were possible every woman, and that your wife
is merely the nearest available representative of the sex you
detest. If that is the case, then Mr. Block's solution, offering
a virtually infinite series of indistinguishable victims for
slaughter and decapitation, will no doubt attract you—if not
as a practical plan of action then as an agreeable fantasy for
the beguilement of your hours of idleness.

But in that event I must ask you, I fear, to excuse me
from communicating further with you on this or any other
matter: since I am a woman I must presume myself to be
included among the objects of your detestation, and I should
not, in those circumstances, feel able to maintain, even at a
distance, that minimum semblance of amiability which is required for civilized discourse.

You will say, perhaps, that I am making too much of
the matter. To imagine the pleasures of killing me and cutting me up in bits is not, you will say, a sign of any particular

152

ill will toward me, you intend no unkindness by it—it is murder in jest, mutilation in jest, no offense in the world—and surely I am not so unsportsmanlike as to take it personally? But I do, Tim, I do—I take it damned personally, and in devilish bad part.

But forgive me—I have no evidence for imputing to you such a motive as I have mentioned: the fantasy is Mr. Block's, not yours. Should he offer further admonishment on the state of your psyche, bid him look first to his own. Assuming, as I trust I may, that his solution is as repugnant to you as it is to me, mine is the only one left. I take this opportunity to enclose a copy of the program for the next Edinburgh Festival, and remain yours as sincerely as ever.

FROM LAWRENCE BLOCK

*I*t's all right. I forgive you.

But I must say I was furious with you for a while there. Your second letter had me snarling and snapping and ready to break all my furniture into kindling And, I must admit, it was largely my own fault. You made things nixonially clear in your initial correspondence. "Dear friends," you began. Somehow my eye missed the letter *S*. Somehow my *amour-propre* led me to assume, not that I was your only friend, but that I was the sole person to be consulted about the particular problem at hand. You had sketched out a problem. I proposed, rather skillfully I must say, a solution. You would either put the solution into practice or (as I rather expected) acknowledge its brilliance while admitting your own psychic incapacity to carry it out. I was prepared to find either response gratifying.

Then your second communication reached me. "Dear friends," it began. The first sentence made certain that I took note of the plural: "Frankly I was shocked by the five letters I received . . ."

Shocked, were you? No more than I was by the news that you had consulted four other admittedly lesser talents for help. I could see your going to them after having received my reply. Aware that you lacked the strength of character to follow the plan I'd sketched out, you might explore other alternatives before giving the thing up altogether. Or, for that matter, I could understand your having made the rounds of my four colleagues *before* coming to me; when their advice proved worthless, you would then have come to the person whose counsel you should have sought in the first place.

But to have gone to us all at the same time! I can only suppose you thought it more efficient that way, like the young woman who slept with nine men in the hope of having a baby in a month. I was frankly infuriated, with you and with myself. How could you have had the effrontery to ask me to enter some sort of sweepstakes, preparing an elaborate (and damned sensible) plan for homicide and tossing it into a fishbowl, hoping my proposal might be drawn as the winning entry?

Has he no idea, I thundered, how long I have occupied a preeminent position in my field? Has he no sense of my stature in my profession? Does the bugger think I write on spec?

Doesn't he know who I am?

Ah, ego, ego. If it's conscience that makes cowards of us all, surely it's ego that makes of us buffoons. Still, one must not be too quick to denigrate the ego. It is, after all, the only thing that separates us from the saints.

But I digress.

If I was mad at you, think how furious I was with myself.

How could I have missed the obvious implication of your first letter? Rereading it, I wondered at my own narrowness of vision. It was abundantly clear that you were seeking assistance from several of us, and I don't know how I failed to spot it right away.

It's just as well. Had I known, I would have tossed your initial missive in the round file, along with the offers of cut-price luggage and magazine subscriptions. You would have had to choose your murder method from the contributions of Mr. Westlake, Mr. Lovesey, Mr. Hillerman, and Ms. Caudwell. It's an ill wind and all that, and in this instance I should think all the good would be blown to your wife, who might reasonably expect to live on into her second century.

My first impulse, I must admit, was to toss out their contributions unread. I have for years been doing just that with their novels, which their publishers persist in sending me in the hope of eliciting promotional blurbs. A word from me, evidently, goes a long way in establishing a lesser writer's reputation, and I'm continuously besieged with galleys from hopeful editors. I have thus long since formed my opinion of the work of Westlake, Lovesey, Hillerman, and Caudwell, and could well imagine what sort of murder they would lay out for you.

Westlake would enlist the aid of some bumbling criminals, and he'd have all of them try to kill your wife, and they'd all fail, until she died laughing. Lovesey would have her slain in the ring by a bare-knuckled pugilist. Hillerman would dress you up in a feather headdress and have you make a sand painting, calling down the Great Spirit to crush your wife to death in a buffalo stampede. And Caudwell would shuttle you between Lincoln's Inn and the Isles of

Greece, in the company of people named Ragweed and Catnip.

It was with this attitude that I sat down with their manuscripts and read them in turn. And, I have to say, I was greatly surprised. All four of these worthies attained a level of logic and clarity, and indeed of imagination and creativity, which I have never observed in their fiction. Perhaps they missed their true calling, perhaps they ought years ago to have taken a different direction vocationally, perhaps they might even now be writing marketing programs for major corporations. That's by the way; they're all of them too long in the tooth for new careers, and one can only hope the ingenuity and resourcefulness they've displayed in the present undertaking will someday find its way into their novels.

I read the manuscripts in the order you yourself received and read them. First was Westlake's.

Impressive!

Oh, his response was a little slow getting off the ground, with all of that tedious instruction in the art of setting up a false identity. I would hardly think the process needs so much in the way of spelling out, given the considerable amount of media attention the topic has drawn in recent years, including a segment some time ago on "60 Minutes." Such a wealth of unnecessary detail suggests that Westlake has not forgotten his days writing for two cents a word, where nothing was told in a sentence that could be stretched to a paragraph. Perhaps those days are not so far behind him.

Still, once Minor DeMortis had been called into existence, Westlake's scheme had much to recommend it. The nicest touch, certainly, lay in the fact that your false friend Blazes would know exactly who had dropped him in the shit, and how. You shoot your wife, you hand him the gun, and there he is, holding the murder weapon, his hand full of nitrite particles, with the corpse stretched out beside him.

Then, while Blazes tries to explain, you manage the neat turn of providing your own alibi. This is all very Westlakean, isn't it? One envisions a stage farce, with the hero emerging from one door even as another is slamming behind him, now wearing a wig, now wearing an eye patch, now tall, now short. The DeMortis persona, seen only by police and strangers in another city, will not draw that intense a glance. It is, Westlake argues, a deception that can be successfully maintained.

I wonder. The same policemen will have questioned you and your alter ego DeMortis on the same evening. Even if we assume that you are a master of disguise, even if you can vary your facial expression and the pitch of your voice, are you prepared to stake your life, your wife's fortune, and your sacred honor on the premise that not one of those cops will smell a rat in sheep's clothing? It might work, I'll allow that much, but you in turn must allow that it leaves a lot to chance.

So too does the scheduling. The cops question you. You will spend the night, you tell them, and return home in the morning. Meanwhile, they may establish your alibi by consulting with your friend DeMortis.

Off they go, looking for DeMortis. And off you go, looking to *be* DeMortis.

Fine, but where's the margin for error? "Come with us and help us find DeMortis," they say. And how, pray tell, do you handle that?

For the sake of argument, I'm willing to assume that it does all get handled, that the unlikely deception fools everyone, and that your alibi stands up. It will ultimately fall apart, however, not in the light of police investigation but in that of the private investigation which your friend Blazes will commission.

If Westlake's strength is that Blazes knows who framed him, there too is Westlake's weakness. Armed with this knowledge, Blazes will know whom to attack. He will unquestionably engage a team of detectives, who will know that your alibi has to be false. They will accordingly go looking for Minor DeMortis, and either they will not find him or they will readily pierce his disguise.

Then they will begin to pick your alibi apart. They will go to the restaurant where you had your sumptuous post-murder dinner. They will interview the captain, the waiter, the busboy. They will examine the check and the charge slip. They will conclude that you dined alone.

They will fall on you like a ton of bricks. Even Westlake, himself a few bricks shy of a load, can scarcely claim otherwise.

And it has to happen this way. Blazes has to attack your alibi. Once attacked, it has to fall apart. It is a Potemkin village, all false front. Peer at it for an instant from other than the intended angle and it ceases utterly to deceive.

I'll tell you something. It's just as well. Because, for all its ingenuity, for all the slick superficiality which is so characteristic of Westlake's work, it lacks one of your requirements. You wanted a murder which would make the world stop and take notice. This one would lead the world to shrug and turn its attention elsewhere.

Because what does it amount to? A lover kills his mistress and is speedily apprehended. Kills her by shooting her.

Ho fucking hum.

The artistry, you see, is all concealed. The only person who will know that this is anything but the most humdrum of homicides is Blazes himself, who will react by tearing down the façade. At that point, I admit, your ingenuity will become apparent to one and all, but only by placing you in the dock for murder.

Not quite as you would want it, I shouldn't think.

And now for Lovesey.

If Westlake characteristically began by padding out his narrative, Lovesey as characteristically opened by putting the whole thing in historical perspective. His most nearly satisfactory works are set in the Victorian era. They're more convincing than his contemporary tales, perhaps because we aren't in as good a position to realize that he doesn't know what he's talking about.

The references to Smith and Haigh, then, got me off to a bad start. So, too, did Lovesey's monetary demands. "An annuity of let us say a million dollars for the rest of my life." (Does he mean a million a year? Or does he ask no more than a million-dollar annuity, which should pay out a respectable annual sum? It is characteristically unclear, isn't it?)

I must say that it never occurred to me to ask you for money. I was happy enough to be able to offer a suggestion which might prove useful. I can only guess that Lovesey, unlikely ever to earn a substantial sum from his fiction, saw his one shot at wealth through persuading you to part with some of yours. If you did pay him such a sum, I suspect the crass bastard would never write another word.

Hmmmm. I know a million dollars is a lot of money, but maybe you ought to give it some thought. . . .

But, once again, I digress. All of these considerations aside, I am forced to admit that Lovesey's scenario is nothing short of brilliant. It is bizarre, it is theatrical, and it is even alliterative. *The Jellyfish in the Jacuzzi* indeed. The man has a knack, and it is clear, is it not, that he missed his calling? All these years he would have been so much better employed writing headlines for the tabloids.

We cannot fault Lovesey's crime as we did Westlake's. Here, to be sure, is a crime which will not waste its piscine fragrance on the desert air. If everything artful about Westlake's scheme was below the surface, Lovesey's is very much the reverse. His murder is very much such stuff as headlines are made of.

As a matter of fact, his crime will make headlines before anyone has been murdered. Even as you are laying the groundwork, your efforts will be getting a considerable amount of attention, first from your friends, then from the national press.

There's the problem.

"I want to see you on the front page of every paper in America," Lovesey has written. I don't know that a houseful of finned vermin will quite accomplish this feat, but it will come close. "There will be intense speculation as to which of your friends could have pulled such an elaborate trick," he goes on. Indeed there will be, and the press, obliging publicists for your efforts, will not leave it at that. They will interview. They will investigate. They will stick their long journalistic noses into every nook and cranny. If you have laid a trail which will successfully implicate Blazes as the practical joker, his role will come to light long before there is a sea wasp in the whirlpool. More likely than not, they will probe beyond the false trail you have laid and establish that you played this practical joke upon yourself.

At which point, sir, you will be on the front pages again, looking like the greatest horse's ass that ever lived. Having already been the butt of a bizarre practical joke, you will have emerged as the witless practical joker himself. Your wife, you may be sure, will join heartily in the general laughter.

What to do? Shoot her, I'd say. You'll get off. Given the stunts you've pulled, people will be quick to assume that you were aiming at your own foot, and the shot went wide.

Even if all this doesn't happen—and it will, it will—even, I say, if you manage everything, Lovesey's scenario depends upon other people following an extremely arbitrary script. Suppose your wife passes on the Chocolate Binge, deciding that she has other fish to fry, as it were. Suppose she goes, and finds out the date is wrong, and spends the night anyway? Suppose she comes home and, for any number of reasons, decides to pass on the Jacuzzi? Suppose the poor sea wasp, moved one time too many, expires in its new home? (Sea wasps don't travel at all well, you know.) Suppose—but I could list no end of suppositions, and that's the point, you see. Altogether too much is left to chance. Lovesey's plan might work as fiction—fanciful, improbable, sillier-than-life fiction—but it's no way to disencumber oneself of a real wife in real life.

To drive a final nail into Lovesey's coffin, consider the two chaps who serve as exemplars at the beginning of his narrative. George Joseph Smith and John George Haigh indeed. Why do you suppose we know their names? Because they got away with it?

Case closed, I'd say.

*   *   *

And now for Hillerman.

What an impressive scheme he has worked out here! It was hardly what I would have expected. I anticipated another earnest effort, a plodding narrative full of conflicted tribal police officers and insensitive Caucasians, with the murder pinned on Lo, the poor Indian. I thought surely I'd pick up some arcane bit of Zuñi lore, something that would stay with me long after the reading experience itself was happily forgotten. I never expected such sheer cleverness from Hillerman, and I take my war bonnet off to him.

It could work, too. There's a good deal of charm to the notion, certainly, of making yourself the most obvious suspect, and indeed of disarming the police by confessing right off the bat, leaving it to them to prove you innocent. It has worked time and time again in the fiction of writers every bit as resourceful as Hillerman, so why should it not work in real life?

The answer, I fear, lies in the complaint Hillerman himself makes in his opening pages. Crime is unimaginative, and only the dullest criminals get caught, and in the dullest manner possible. The police, perhaps in response, have become quite dull, and while the tools for forensic investigation grow ever more acute, they are employed in an increasingly slipshod manner.

A few years ago, for example, a woman's body was recovered from the Hudson River and an autopsy performed by the New York medical examiner's office determined that she had drowned. One of the personnel in the office, more playful than most, wound up keeping the severed skull as a desk ornament. (I am not making this up.) Months later, someone idly examining the skull noted for the first time

164

there was a bullet in it. The woman had not drowned. She had been shot in the head.

Hillerman would have us assume that the police, having been presented with a dead woman in a bathtub and a husband who readily admits clouting her and holding her head underwater, will look further. It is unquestionably true that a careful postmortem examination would turn up inconsistencies, but how careful an autopsy do you suppose you're going to get?

Your wife is rich and prominent, so perhaps caution and attention to detail would be the order of the day. (The woman with the bullet in the skull was monied and socially prominent, too, and her husband and murderer was a doctor. So one can take nothing for granted.) Let us assume, at any rate, that the autopsy would disclose what you would wish it to. The problem, then, is one of taking the noose which has just fallen from your own neck and fastening it around Boylan's.

It all goes well in Hillerman's script. You say this, the cop says that, you say thus, the cop says so, you say ee-ther, the cop says eye-ther—neat, isn't it?

I don't know that it would play that way.

I could say more, a great deal more, to dissuade you from pursuing the course of action Hillerman proposes. But did you ever happen to read a short story of mine called *The Ehrengraf Nostrum?* In it, the titular hero Martin Ehrengraf is called upon to defend a client who has seemingly murdered a whole host of strangers through product tampering, all with the aim of disposing of a spouse in the process.

I don't know if you're familiar with the story. I'm rather more certain, however, that Mr. Hillerman is familiar with

165

it, and my attorney seems quite sanguine about the possibility of a successful plagiarism suit.

Accordingly, on advice of counsel I'll say no more about Hillerman's delightful proposal.

Finally, Sarah Caudwell.

Once I got past the florid gush of the woman's prose, I was quite overwhelmed by the glittering brilliance of Caudwell's scenario. Her scheme is quite simple, yet highly stylized and unquestionably dramatic. All efforts aim at producing that one unparalleled moment, when Blazes is apprehended over your wife's dead body with the murder weapon in his hand.

It is a grabber, this murder. It would go down in the annals of crime even if the actual circumstances were never to become known. Reading it, I several times pursed my lips to emit a soundless whistle. When I reached the end, I winced.

Why, this is quite excellent, I told myself. And eminently workable. And perhaps, I thought, ever quick to give credit where due, perhaps this is even better than my own proposal.

And yet, and yet.

The taped scream could be a problem. If the recording should come to light, if you are not able to retrieve the tape machine and get rid of it, the game is up. For you to do so requires perfect timing and demands that nothing whatsoever go wrong. Indeed, the entire scheme has that caveat, doesn't it?

A minor cavil, that. I brushed it aside as unworthy. There was, I decided, nothing wrong with Caudwell's plan.

But why did I hesitate to embrace it wholeheartedly?

I slept on it, and in the morning the answer was clear.

With the new day's dawn, I could look at the Caudwell opus and see the serpent under it. There you'd be, staging an elaborate murder thousands of miles from home. I can see you now, telling your guests there is something you have forgotten to tell your wife about the next morning's arrangements, and excusing youself for a few moments. And hurrying to her room, and knocking on the door, and, when there is no response, letting yourself in.

"You still have your key," Caudwell writes. Interesting, is it not, that she takes the trouble to point that out? You still have your key, and you use it and throw open the door, and what do you find?

Not, I shouldn't think, your wife, waiting patiently to be killed. No, my friend, I fear you will walk in on something else entirely. A hired assassin who will stab you in the heart. A chambermaid, cruelly used and more cruelly slain, with your dagger in her heart. I can't say precisely what you will encounter because I can't guess precisely what Miss Caudwell will have arranged for you, but I am sure it will be a surprise, and I rather doubt it will be a happy one.

Do you see what you have done? You have engaged a woman to help you murder your wife. Oh, the towering folly of it! If Caudwell has her way you will be twice hoist, first on your own petard, then on the gibbet.

"I hope I may claim without boasting to have provided the climax that I promised you," the cheeky bitch writes. "I do not know if you will find it as satisfying as you expected."

Indeed.

As you can see, I was more than a little impressed with all four members of what I found myself thinking of as the backup crew. They had greatly exceeded expectations, and if each fell a little short of the mark, well, what of it? I was reasonably certain you would have little trouble in seeing the clear superiority of my scheme and would proceed forthwith.

Then I read your second letter with some attention, read it clear through this time.

At first I was greatly alarmed. Here you were, rushing to put Westlake's plan in motion, and carrying it one toke over the line by making DeMortis into a girl! This man, I thought, this would-be criminal genius, has just been looking for an excuse to put on women's clothes. Scratch an uxoricide, find a drag queen.

I was still recovering from the shock when you had abandoned Diana Clement to chase down Lovesey's plan. And what do I find you doing but littering your own lawn with giant crabs.

Suddenly the crabs are gone. Is a call to 911 all it takes to get such creatures swept from one's yard? You must live in a superior neighborhood. The crabs are gone, then, and I find you hunting mushrooms, eventually turning up one that will leave bodies contorted into alphabetical shapes. Do you hope to have your victims spell out a dying message? If you poison an infinite number of monkeys, will they spell out all of Shakespeare's plays?

The mushrooms are tossed—with a little oil and garlic, I presume—when Caudwell's Scottish idyll arrives. You begin to execute her plan, only to abandon it when my letter reaches you. And I read how you begin to carry out the steps I've outlined for you, only to lay off when a chance remark of your wife's returns your attention once more to the Westlake procedure.

I almost washed my hands of you at this point. I almost

bought the image you were so cleverly trying to sell us, of a dilatory dilettante, unable to stick to anything for any length of time, helplessly addicted to embroidering everything at hand until it was so overladen with needlework that one could see none of the whole cloth under it. "To hell with him," I may have said aloud. "He is a bumbler and a time waster, he could not kill a fly, and writing further to him would only be throwing good paper after bad."

Then I read one section a second time.

Interestingly, in your preliminary attempts to execute my proposal, you perpetrated no embroidery whatsoever. You gathered some body hairs and sundry bits of corporal residue, and that, on the face of it, is all you did.

I purchased newspapers from your city, back issues from the previous two weeks. I read. A scant three days before the date of your second letter, a young woman had been horribly murdered at a local motel. She seems to have gone to the room, registered to a Mr. J. G. Haigh, in response to a telephone call; she herself was employed as an outcall masseuse.

The woman, a Ms. Thelma Rackowski, seems to have been strangled. It must have been a difficult matter examining the throat for ligature, however, as part of that organ reposed on the bed with her body while the other was attached to her head, which had been mounted upon one of the wall lamps. (The shade had been removed, the head forced neck-down onto the bulb. Was the bulb lit? Did light shine out of her mouth, like a jack-o'-lantern? The newspaper story lacked detail.)

Other portions of the young lady's anatomy had been artfully removed, with various portions placed in curious juxtaposition to one another.

I called the police in your town. Knowing they would keep certain clues from the press, I avoided representing myself as a journalist. Instead, I passed myself off as a state police officer from a state five hundred miles distant. I allowed that the Rackowski homicide had some touches in common with a recent series of murders in our own bailiwick. Had the killer left any physical evidence behind?

Indeed he had, I learned. A careful investigation had turned up an array of body hair, some of which could have been previously present in the room, spotless housekeeping not being a trademark of the motel in question. Several hairs, however, had been recovered from the body of the victim, including a pubic hair which had depended from the young woman's lower lip. It was not one of the victim's own hairs, I was told, and had been tentatively determined to have been supplied by a male Caucasian.

I could have put a name to that male Caucasian, couldn't I?

By the time I terminated the call, I had taken care to establish several cardinal differences between the homicides I was presumably investigating and the work of the Motel Ripper. Once I'd hung up I no longer needed to hide my jubilation. Had I been wearing a hat, I'd have taken it off to you. Hell, I'd have tossed it in the air.

You were following my plan!

And how clever you were to have pretended to put my colleagues' plans into operation, botching them all the while. You'll understand, won't you, if I allow myself to revel in your accomplishment? I bear no ill will for the late Ms. Rackowski, to be sure. Nor do I have anything against your wife, or your friend Boylan. Even so, their deaths and indeed the deaths of whatever other innocent victims perish along the way cannot fail to bring me a certain unwholesome but undeniable satisfaction.

You can't blame me, can you, for surrendering to the pride of authorship?

I thought not.

FROM DONALD E. WESTLAKE

DEAR FRIEND,

S o. You're beginning to enjoy our correspondence, are you? That may change, my *friend*.
Granted, I had understood from the outset that you were adding to your risk of exposure by consulting others as well as myself—yet another indication of your ambivalence toward the entire operation—but I had expected you would be forming a jury of at least my, if not your, peers. The latest Ted Bundy or John Wayne Gacy, say. Dr. Hannibal Lecter. Pol Pot. Imelda Marcos. A member of the Senate's Intelligence Oversight Committee. An executive from Drexel Burnham. People, in other words, who had *already* gotten away with murder. I'd thought, quite naturally, you understood that my own . . .

Well. Never mind. The point is, I had no idea at the outset that you intended to insult me in such a fashion; to cobble me together with these, these *scriveners*. I had no thought that you expected me to hobnob, rub elbows, shuffle along with the likes of these makeweights, these cutpennies, these *artificers*.

173

Well, it's not their fault, I mustn't blame them overly. They've done their best, poor catchpoles, and I shall give them—not you, my *friend*, them—the decent respect of treating their humble offerings with sympathetic patience and a critical eye well tempered by compassion for human imperfectibility.

(Though I freely admit that the thought of their being invited to criticize, pass judgment on, grade, and rate *me* galls rather severely. I grind my teeth at the prospect, as though at the sight of a fine lace antimacassar in the paws of Sylvester Stallone. Which is only one of the reasons, my *friend*, why I have chosen to . . . Well, never mind. We'll get to all that, in good time.)

Are you comfortable? Where you sit reading this missive, I mean. Are you comfy now? Have you chosen to read in the music room downstairs, with its tacky Mafia-like red flocked wallpaper? Or in your cream-and-gold dressing room upstairs, with the child-porn videos in the bottom left locked drawer of the Louis XV commode? Wherever you've chosen to settle with this communication, I do hope you're comfortable. For now. No drafts on the back of your neck? No discomfiting itch at your elbows? No uneasy sense of eyes watching, observing your every movement? Good. Read on.

Being a gentleman—I am always a gentleman, fortunately for you—I shall begin with the lady's contribution. The flaws in this proposal glare brightly enough, I should think, for even you to see them, though the hugger-mugger with the dirk and the cassette player has a certain *jeu de paume* which would no doubt have a certain appeal for frivolous minds; the sort of people who can never guess the ending of a "Columbo" episode.

But what of the blood? This skene-dhu you're waggling

about with such amateurish abandon will surely sever some artery, some primal blood canal. Have you ever been to the stockyards? Stabbing victims bleed prodigiously, my *friend*, they spout, they spew, they gush, they fountain over, and over everything in sight. With every desperate final beat of their hearts, these doomed wretches disembogue yet another hot sticky stream of the stuff, in an arching carmine torrent. Are you really agile enough to dance out of the way of that flood, encased as you are in that unfamiliar and unflattering costume? And even if you could scamper lithely aside, a homicidal Baryshnikov, what of the tape recorder? You must secrete it in your wife's blood-soaked garments without getting blood on yourself and without jamming the mechanism of the machine with gore. And then you must reclaim it! Hide it on your person without leaving a single stain!

Ho ho. May I watch?

But this isn't even the primary difficulty with the operation. No, the primary difficulty is simply stated: If you leave your home, your neighborhood, your nation, and go to some foreign land, you will be *a fish out of water*.

Anyone who chooses to commit a murder on alien soil had best be in uniform and at war; otherwise, the unknowns are just too many. You can have no idea, ahead of time, what customs, characteristics, local eccentricities may confound your plotting.

And if this is true generally when away from home, it is doubly true in the British Isles, where the illusion of a shared language creates the dangerous impression that you understand what's going on. You do not. Behavior which may seem to you perfectly innocuous could raise eyebrows and suspicion along those cleared moors, could make you an object of more than cursory observation even before you make your blood-soaked move. You'll never know what nuances you're getting wrong, what subtle clues of national character and local arcanity you are leaving in your wake, spoor that Scottish policemen would fall on with that dour glee and guilt-ridden doggedness and blunt-minded persistence that has made the race of Scots such feared bores wherever in the world their rotten bagpiping has sounded.

That chauvinism is fatal to clarity of thought should go without saying. That Ms. Caudwell's invitation to your ruin reeks of it does go without saying. Go without it.

In fact, the only good thing to be said for this first suggestion is that when you are caught—and you will be caught—you will be tried in a Scottish court. You have the money to hire the finest barristers and solicitors. There is a finding available to you in Scotland unlike the possible conclusions to a criminal trial in virtually any other jurisdiction in the world, where the choices are usually between Guilty and Not Guilty. In Scotland, and nowhere else in the British Isles, and in fact nowhere else in the civilized world, there is a third possible conclusion: Not Proven. It has been said, with some accuracy, that Not Proven means, "You didn't do it, and don't do it again."

Well, of course, unless you remarry you won't be able to do it again, will you? And surely your pricey Edinburgh legal servants will find a way to steer you through the Not Proven door.

Still, that's hardly a particularly artistic finish to your endeavor, to be sneered at by old duffers in white wigs who speak as though tree roots had been implanted between their teeth. But if that's your idea of a grand exit, go right ahead.

Or perhaps it is Mr. Hillerman's plan you'd prefer, even though, in my initial letter to you, I pointed out what was wrong with that whole approach. If I may quote from myself (I only quote from those I deeply admire):

"My dear sir, *you studied to be a doctor!* Don't you think the police will investigate your background? They will, I assure you, and do so much more exhaustively, I may say, than you have offered it up to inspection in your letter to me. If the police are presented with a woman dead by poisoning, whose husband had once studied to be a doctor, they will not for a second be duped or distracted, not by all the false trails and false alibis in the world. Your cleverness, plus mine, plus as much more cleverness as you can bring into play from other sources, will all be wasted against the blunt wall of their conviction. And yours; for murder."

Well, so much for "as much cleverness as you can bring into play from other sources," eh? Of course, at that time, I had no idea of the composition of the group with which you intended me to consort. It's only since then that I've realized I must . . .

Well, never mind that. The point is poison. A bit after the advice I have just cited, I made the point again, and even more bluntly: "[I]f you once upon a time studied to be a doctor, leave the poison on the shelf." I can hardly be clearer than that.

But even if your personal medical background were limited to overstatement of insurance claims, Mr. Hillerman's advice would still be fatally flawed. You wanted one perfect murder; he gives you a bargain basement of manufacturers' seconds.

Can there be an artistic mass murder? Mass murder, by its very nature, is not art but kitsch. It displaces nuance with sensation, individual craftsmanship with cheap mass production methods, specific impulse with generalized marketing strategy. You have asked for caviar-to-the-few and Mr. Hillerman has responded with Egg-McMuffin-to-the-many. Of course, if you *want* a Venus de Milo with a clock in her stomach, go right ahead. After all, Mr. Hillerman's exercise is not without its antic charm. The whole business of rushing into a bathroom to murder an already-murdered wife, confessing it at once to the police, all that rutabaga is quite endearing. One can see where you might be tempted to play such a part.

But wait; not quite so soon. The inadequacies of this scheme have not as yet been exhaustively tolled. There is the matter of the by-products of Mr. Hillerman's version of your crime, by which I mean that slag heap, as it were, of eighteen bodies, stacked like so many Yule logs, mushroomed in their prime. He does not give much consideration to those eighteen shells of blighted hopes, those foreshortened shadows, disturbed dreams, does not give them much consideration in any sense of the term, but if you are to be the one who drop-kicks them through God's goalposts, my *friend*, if you are to be in the most final sense their man from Porlock, it behooves you to get to know these people, and to know them well.

Why? They are nothing to you, am I correct? Merely a smokescreen, a diversion. Eighteen human lives, snuffed for a sleight-of-hand. Standards *are* slipping.

But let us pause a moment in our headlong self-satisfaction, let us focus our attention on these eighteen souls as they shuffle disconsolately from the stage of life, all together crowding into the wings for their wings. Who are they? Is it possible to know anything about them?

As a matter of fact, it is. They are a part of the clientele of something called the Yummie Yuppie Deli, where they purchase, among other things, exotic mushrooms. We can presume from this that all or most of the eighteen will be well educated, well off and fairly young; under forty. With living parents, for the most part.

This is not a case of the burning to the ground of a nursing home full of ancients who had already lived their lives, run their races, worn their laurel wreaths. These are people on the rising curve of life, people whose successes so far are merely precursors of the triumphs sure to be ahead, people whose families and significant others are excessively, dotingly, mawkishly proud of them; perhaps even living their own lives vicariously through these superpersons' accomplishments.

How many of those families, how many of those significant others, will not be satisfied with the rather hurried latticework Mr. Hillerman has placed around your connection with the affair? How many will have the money, the interest, the grief, the rage, the irritation, and the time to hire private detectives? How long will it take before your town begins to fill up with these creatures?

(Private detectives are, despite popular belief, distressingly easy to pick out of a crowd. They look like unemployed parking lot attendants, and they have bad breath. Also, their pockets are filled with small pieces of paper containing hurriedly scrawled notes.)

Yes, that's the future you can look forward to, should you choose the Hillerman scenario. Twenty or thirty scruffy, hungry, completely unscrupulous private detectives sniffing away at your trail. Even assuming the police accept the ludicrous notion of the innocence of a former medical student in the poisoning death of his wife, you will still have that Boschian army all over you like leeches in a swamp.

179

Remember this about private detectives. They have no ethics, and no morals. They are not bound by the rules of evidence, as the police are. They are not bound by any rules. They are not above manufacturing evidence to earn their paltry pay. Success is their only criterion, accomplishment their only option.

They will eat you alive.

So perhaps you'll turn to Mr. Block's option. If so, it means you haven't been reading with sufficient attention till now, and should go back to the beginning and study my words more heedfully. I'll wait, *friend*. I have all the time you'll need.

Yes, now you understand. My objection to Mr. Hillerman's essay into mass murder holds equally true of the grisly swath Mr. Block would have you cut. In fact, I object even more strenuously to Mr. Block's prescription, as being not merely kitsch but sordid kitsch. It is true, I admit, that the victims Mr. Block has chosen for you are less likely to raise the kind of hue and cry I suggested might ensue in a landscape littered with poisoned yuppies, but surely that isn't the only consideration.

Art is the ennobling of the human experience, the concordance of our species' dreams, fears, ambitions, histories. Squalor without pity is no more than squalor; barren soil for the nurturing of art. At least Mr. Hillerman's broad strokes cut down a band of worthies, folk whose untimely cutting-off contains within it the potential for tragedy, or irony, or *some* component of art. But all these Baggies full of pubic hair, all these assignations with fallen drabs!

Really, sir, your history, your tastes, your current life-style, all suggest not the slightest hint of *nostalgie de la boue*. (Yes, of course, I've found you, despite your pseudonyms, your indirect methods of sending and receiving correspondence. This is the sort of expertise you expected me to have, isn't it? The sort that led you to me in the first place, the sort that for some reason seems to have encouraged you to insult and denigrate me until now I must . . . Well, never mind, we'll get to that. The point at this moment is that I have been observing you for some little time, have learned your habits and the round of your days, have studied you when you thought you were alone . . . Now, for instance. And I know the Block design—freezers full of fingers, noses nesting in ice cube trays, *really!*—is not for you.)

Not that it's a method without attraction, without its uses for someone of a more adamantine cast. It is true that the police, being in general not overeducated, possess a mystic awe of science in all its forms, and particularly forensic science. Give the "lab boys" something to do and the coppers will stand about with their mouths hanging open, and then will go arrest whomever the physical evidence points at; usually to find the case lost a year later, when the jury, unable to understand the expert witnesses, and reacting in normal human fashion to aggravated irritation and boredom, finds the perp Not Guilty.

So there is potential value in Mr. Block's mad method, but what he has given you is an off-the-rack solution, while what you need is something tailor-made. Yes. You need someone like me, who knows you and has found where you live and has any number of ideas precisely tailored to suit no one but you. You, my *friend.*

But what about Mr. Lovesey? He does share Mr. Block's obsession with human hair, but in a slightly more discreet fashion, so the hair fetish in this instance need not cause us as much concern from an artistic point of view. The stage business with the Blu-Tak and the keys is quite decorative; I find myself admiring it. Whether or not death by sea wasp counts as a poisoning—which would therefore be off limits for you (see previous citation of much more previous warning)—is a question I have not as yet entirely resolved to my own satisfaction. But of this much I am certain, however: Mr. Lovesey places more reliance on chance than the maddest Gamblers Anonymous dropout planing toward Las Vegas.

What lucky breaks does Mr. Lovesey absolutely require for his plan to succeed? You must be seen by no one you know on either the plane to the city prior to the murder or the later plane from the city once the Jacuzzi has been baited. You must be seen by no inquisitive person at the lab as you carry a sloshing bucket of sea wasp out the door. Blazes must not have found his own uses for his automobile that afternoon. The maid must not see you in the house, nor clean the Jacuzzi after you leave.

If you did possess luck at such an extraordinary level, my *friend,* you wouldn't need sea wasps or mushrooms or skene-dhus or nipple-clippers at all. You'd need merely to leave the window open behind your wife's place at dinner one evening, in that rather long narrow dining room in your house, with the oddly attractive hutch on the west wall, and a stray breeze could be counted upon to create a draft that would surely carry the woman off with advanced pneumonia before the savory.

(Yes, of course I've been in your home, several times, while installing certain . . . Well, never mind. We'll get to all that later.)

But this madly optimistic dependence on chance isn't the only thing—nor the worst thing—wrong with Mr. Lovesey's offering. To sum up the principal defect in his suggestion with one word, the flaw is one of *character*. Both yours, and his.

Yours first. You say you are a fisherman, but we all know the kind of fisherman you are: more given to tall tales than hard work. One of the least attractive of your characteristics, my *friend*—and there are many unattractive facets to you, in all—is your tendency to repeat jokes, anecdotes, stories, and gag lines. You may have noticed the difference yourself: when other people tell jokes, the surrounding audience laughs; when you tell a joke, the surrounding audience grinds its teeth. They've heard it before.

Think back. What is it you invariably say when some acquaintance of yours has been on a fishing expedition? You wait until someone else asks, "What did you catch?" and then you answer, "Cold," and cover the ensuing sound of the gnashing of teeth with your own braying laugh. For you, at this point in your self-satisfied life, to suddenly become a fevered fisherman would itself be so fishy that suspicion would fall on you even before you'd done anything. What's he up to? everyone would wonder. And then the practical jokes would begin. Guess where the fingers would point.

But, as I said, yours is not the only character that makes this kismet-blessed scheme inadvisable to the point of impossibility. There is Mr. Lovesey's character, as well.

Why *his* character? What does he have to do with your business, once he has completed his task as consulting expert? I invite you to look at that letter of his again for just a moment, *friend*. Have you ever seen such naked greed? Do you really believe the annuity he demands will satisfy him?

Consider the possibilities. Let us assume for just an instant here that Mr. Lovesey is not entirely trustworthy where you're concerned. (He seems awfully willing to let you trust to luck, remember. There isn't a blind curve on the road at which he doesn't want you to pass a truck.) Let us assume he has retained a copy of his letter to you, in which a few words have been altered, to make it clear to anyone reading it—the police, say, just as a for instance—that you had convinced him your intentions were only theoretical, that this was merely a game, and not deadly earnest. And let us assume further that, despite the air of fun involved, his copy of the letter includes a warning from Mr. Lovesey that you must on no account ever put any of his suggestions into effect.

Good so far? Now let us assume you choose Mr. Lovesey's method for ridding yourself of your wife, despite the clarity of my counsel. And let us say that, in fact, blind chance does favor you at every turn, and there you are, the world's richest widower.

And here comes Mr. Lovesey, with a letter he will either sell to you or show to the police.

He'll be harder to dispatch than your wife, *friend*. And who will you turn to for help at that juncture, who will advise you, who will do your planning for you? Not the people you've already rejected, I can tell you that.

No. For reasons both interior and exterior, you'd best leave the sea wasps alone.

But what of my own offering? Let me say that I have seen your Diana Clement, and I must congratulate you on her. She is the kind of refinement of an original script that the very best actors give in performance, discovering their own particular truths within the general truth of a universal story. In that one stroke, changing Minor DeMortis to Diana Clement, you made the story your own, you gave it a compact complexity I can only admire.

(You wanted admiration, as you yourself have pointed out. You shall not gain much of that commodity here below, but here's a bit of it, freely given. I do admire your Diana Clement.)

And just imagine, if you were to be found dead somewhere—oh, say, a stroke, an auto accident, you know the kind of thing—in Diana's fig. The police arrive, the medical personnel, the folk from the mortician. Such surprise! Such confusion! *There's* art, if you want. The laughter of the gods o'erlying a minor everyday human drama.

But there I go again, getting ahead of myself. At this point, I should be explaining why you should choose my little blueprint. (A bit later, I'll explain why you *must* choose it, why it will give you a whole new lease on life. But not yet.)

Well, naturally, the first reason you should choose my plan is that it is the only one without flaw. However, since chance does enter into every human endeavor (and not always as benignly as Mr. Lovesey would suggest), let us admit the possibility that an unlucky break, or even your own clumsiness in following my instructions, leads to your being wanted by the police for questioning in the matter of the offing of your wife. What does my plan afford you that no other plan even considers?

Escape. If all goes agley, my *friend,* you have a built-in escape hatch. While the whole world and his brother hare off in pursuit of the murderous husband, *you become Diana Clement.* (A long-term metamorphosis would have been easier as Minor DeMortis, but your Diana is so good a creation I'd hate to see you give her up. Besides, under the altered conditions of our relationship, you needn't worry overmuch about long-term metamorphoses.)

Additionally, you have made it abundantly clear that a

significant consideration in your mind is that the plan you choose must be at the highest possible level of artistic accomplishment. Here, sir, I offer you neither coincidence nor pubic hair, neither exotic flora nor exotic fauna, no voyages into dangerously unknown terrain, nothing but a graceful arc of invention, employing guile *plus* audacity, talent *plus* technology.

You yourself have described my plan as containing "brazenness," and is that not a hallmark of true art? Art is transformation, my *friend*, and transformation does not exist without brazenness, and willingness to rise above the pedestrian rules and enter the pure realm where the rules have not yet been formalized, where *you* are the rule-bringer, where you are the explorer and the exploration, the artist and the work of art.

For all these reasons, you should choose my plan. But now let me tell you, let me make it perfectly clear to you—do stop squirming in that chair, nothing's going to happen to you now—why you *must* choose it.

The fact is, the thousand abrasions of your excessively abrasive personality I have borne as best I could, but when you ventured upon insult you went too far. I cannot look myself in the mirror ever again, if I let you live. You know now that I know you; who you are, where you are, the habits of your life. You know I have the ingenuity to do you in without the slightest suspicion ever turned in my direction, and I assure you I have the impetus as well. (Forcing me to look up *deipnosophy* is, *by itself,* reason enough.)

But shall I be content to snuff you without having first seen you act out the magnificent plan I have offered? Of course not. So long as I can see that you are moving forward with *my* scheme for doing away with your wife, I shall stay my hand. If, however, I see you take one step toward those jerry-built lesser options, believe me, your end is nigh. Alternatively, if it becomes clear to me you aren't ever going to do for your wife at all, I shall not long remain either patient or bored, I assure you.

So let us assume that, in quite appropriate fear for your life, having been given this additional and even more compelling motive to kill your wife and frame Blazes Boylan, you proceed at a measured—but not too measured—pace, perform the act, escape the clutches of the law, and watch Blazes hustled screaming into the waiting patrol car. What then? Shall I dispatch you in the very moment of your triumph, with Blazes's caterwauling still echoing so pleasantly in your ear?

Of course not. As I pointed out some time earlier, I am a gentleman. I would never be so unsportsmanlike, not even to you. I would leave you to savor your triumph, for some period of time.

Our triumph, I should say. Our triumph, for I shall be savoring it as well. I have before this seen my work in print. I have seen it performed on the stage. I have seen it expressed in film. Now I shall see it on the largest canvas of all, with you my brush. I can expect to feel the afterglow of that moment for quite some time, during which all I will do in your regard is keep an eye on you. I wouldn't want you scampering out of sight, now, would I, like a mouse from some distracted cat? No, no, you shall not get away from *me*.

Eventually, though, memory must fade, pleasure must begin to pall. The moment of triumph will have been experienced to the full. It will be time to move to endgame.

As Mr. Block suggests, this sort of thing could become seductive, even habit-forming. Not your problem, that; you won't be forming any new habits, I don't believe, apart from a tendency to look over your shoulder. Not in the time left you.

Let me assure you, *friend*, nothing in your life will have suited you like the leaving of it. I intend a much more spectacular finish for you than the one we are providing your wife. You shall be *my* work of art, solo, even more brazen, even more ingenious, even more foolproof than the one I have handed you.

You wanted to be a party to the finest example of the perfect murder, murder as a work of art, and so you shall be. Not, perhaps, playing the role you'd hoped for, but how important is that? You will be there, an integral element in the tapestry, an irreplaceable part. Surely you can take pleasure in that thought.

And think of the prospect ahead of you! Months, perhaps even a year or two, engaged magnificently in the most dangerous game. Your final months spiced with danger and accomplishment. And then the finish, at the service of the art you so love. And afterward, *your name* immortally linked to the most gorgeous, the most creative, the most extravagant, the most *perfect* murder of all time!

Why, it's almost enviable.

I'll be seeing you.

FROM TIM

DEAR FRIENDS (and you, too, Mr. Westlake),

*L*et me see if I have this straight. Half the members of the loftiest pantheon of the Mystery Writers Guild are skulking about in their libraries trying to figure out how to cast me in one of their upcoming novels, preferably as the corpse. Among some circles, somewhere, I am certain this is an honor. Now what I've got is this: Mr. Westlake is stamping about my garden bed, taking flight to my high hedges whenever a shadow darkens one of my windows. Is that a cutlass you have in your hand, or a Toledo, or a stiletto, possibly a tomahawk? What is the theme of this denouement? Maybe it's a truncheon or some knuckleduster? A musketoon or a blowgun? A grenade? Or perhaps that is a cup of some Balinese poison you are sloshing about my posies? Be careful, Mr. Westlake: you will no doubt be bumping into Mr. Block in one of his furies, grinding his teeth and tormenting his own entrails, dragging his poleax. Perhaps the two of you can keep company with Messrs. Lovesey and Hillerman en route to an afternoon of hounding my accountant. Ms. Caudwell, no doubt in a mood as bitter as

189

the others, has dressed it up as a kindness—so British—in the form of an invitation to Edinburgh. I suspect that the liveried servants are just now folding down the comforter in my reserved suite at the Bobby Burns Bed 'n' Breakfast, and I am certain that my name has been entered onto the rolls for tomorrow's caber toss. I see her there now, dressed in tartan and tam, squeezing out the baggie's skirl—the famed hospitality of the Scepter'd Isle. Yet somehow I recollect something about the ankle hose of that notorious costume, somewhere near the shoe, a secret sheath of some kind, near the garter flash, for a poniard?

I hesitate to write back for fear that I might drive any of you over the edge—although judging from the mild contempt in which I am held compared to the Olympian loathing each of you directs to the others, I suggest that Mr. Westlake leave off advising me on the condition of my shoulder and scrutinize his own. Lawrence Block lives!

But I do delight in all the preening and swaggering. I am reminded of a story told me by one of the Maddens of Lexington, Kentucky. Keeping up the family tradition, he had trained several thoroughbreds that had won the Derby and the Preakness. Thoroughbreds, whether filly or stallion, are notoriously temperamental. No one, no trainer, no jockey, no one can simply take them to the track and demand that they run. They must be worked up to it, I am told. My friend said that it is best to feed thoroughbreds all alone in a closed stall—so that their equine solipsism may sustain the necessary fiction that he or she is the only horse on earth eating such rare and fine oats, and that the rest of the species might very well be starving to death while this one luxuriates with a snout plunged deep into the feedbag. On race day, the top doors of the stalls are flung open, and all the thoroughbreds are fed together in full view of one another, so that each might feel the dreadful sting of equality. Alas, is there a greater torture? But, my, how they run, each drawing on its own bile, chafing at the noseband and the throatlatch to best the others—although perhaps all the work is simply a vain attempt to flee the painful company of peers. My friend always insisted that he felt a perverse euphoria when he flung open those top doors on race day. I now know this happiness.

My race has produced quite a winner's circle. I have five nearly flawless possibilities, each ornamented in detail as rugged as the Baggie of pubic hair, as excessive as the *Chironex fleckeri,* as complex as a fully created alter ego, as arcane as the skene-dhu, or as psychological as an outright admission of guilt. Each solution stands on its own as a work of art, worthy of an amateur's marveling whether carried out or not. I should like to award each of you the white ribbon and a hearty thank-you-very-much, although someone must get the blue ribbon—but I get ahead of myself.

As an artist, as *the* artist, I cannot tell you how happy I am with your solutions, your *work.* I am even happy as an employer. I only bring up my state by way of contrast to my even greater bliss at the outcome of what might be called the second heat. I am not just talking about the savagery of the prose in the second letters. (I once thought the infamous theater critic for the *New York Times* could be brutal. He is a mere Mr. Rogers in print compared to any of you in a good mood.) But, if we may or may not have succeeded on breathing life into the corpse of murder-as-art (that depends on me now), we have done something even better, something that practically safeguards the original purpose. We have created the equivalent of murder's literary criticism and begun the hard work of establishing a basic aesthetics. I imagine Ph.D. candidates sometime ages and ages hence (you'd better hope) deconstructing these texts to uncover the rudiments of our sensibility.

And I think one does emerge. I was struck at how coherent the critiques were, how consistent. Each of you was taken to task by the others for relying too much, in some way, on serendipity—whether it was Lovesey and his plane schedules, Caudwell's tape recorder, Westlake and his pistol club, Hillerman's dogged and suspicious detective, or Block's false trail of micro-evidence. There must be, always, a degree of the ineffable in a great murder. I think we establish this as the sine qua non of any artful murder, the mere coming together of it all. The simple belief that it will work. Scores painted cathedrals in the Renaissance. But one can imagine only Michelangelo on his scaffolding—no doubt cringing from time to time that his monstrous plan, his arrogant epic, might end up looking like a garish throng of polychromatic peasants, from the distant perspective of the floor, seemingly cross-eyed and lumpen, dewlaps flapping—but believing in the mere chance of his idea, that one image would fit with another, and that the whole would constitute the greatest painting in the world. Modern scientists call this fitting together *contingency*—the importance of fortuitous concatenations. I am told that it is the origin, according to Oriental philosophers and mystical poets, of Buddha's serene smile.

One, I think, simply has to believe that it will work—that the planes will leave on time that day, that the damned cassette recorder will click on when the button is pressed, that Blazes will join the club on cue, that the detective will sense a contradiction in the neat confession, and that the tiny evidence when magnified by forensic technology will appear to be a milewide swath leading to Blazes. One could make a case that the aesthetics of murder are the aesthetics of contingency—the beauty of luck. It is only fitting that an art form that aspires to such high ideals must raise itself above the aesthetics of craft associated with other pursuits. Who wants an art whose beauty is under the complete control of the artist? Who could care for a beauty that would undoubtedly be atomized and sifted into categories of technique and become the subject of soporific seminars at the annual PMLA meeting? Rather, let us have an aesthetics built upon the exacting hand of the artist and the palsied hand of fate, upon talent and faith. I like it.

I suppose I should tremble at writing this letter. But, as I said before, you each have more to fear from one another, than I of you. But I also can't see any of you actually going through with what I comfortably have set out to do—dark, grisly murder. Each of you is certainly outfitted with the proper genius (which I have borrowed, thank you) and the appropriate measure of rage, but each of you lacks the arrogance to push yourself beyond the page and to the knife. It is the difference between, say, Boswell and Johnson.

There is another reason I have little to fear, either as a threat to my life or as a threat of releasing these papers. Mr. Hillerman informs me he has made copies of my acid-soaked notes. Have you, now? And what do you think I have done with yours? Let them decompose in a folder? You threaten to expose me as a murderer, which is what I am. Where is the revelation? I, in turn, threaten to expose each of you as

a murderer's accomplice, which you—at least for now—are
not. No, each of you holds close to your heart the belief that
the laurels of immortality await you. No doubt they do. That
is why I wrote you in the first place. But imagine if the stench
of murder fouled your perfumed reputations? You understand the modern media as well as I do. Television—their
chief engine—makes no distinction between fame and notoriety. Each of you would immediately lose that precious
epithet you have spent a lifetime earning: "Oh, Caudwell.
Oh, Lovesey. Oh, Block. Oh, Westlake. Oh, Hillerman. You
mean, the *writer*!" What if, instead, the rabble of fans were
heard to mutter, "You mean the one who got caught up in
that famous murder?" Your reputation would become a sub-
set of my own.

No, I am not worried. I am protected by a mantle more
lasting than bronze, by a shield harder than any of the flimsy
armaments in the Pentagon's depot. Between me and harm's
way stands the ego of a great writer.

So, I don't think any of you can expect to discover who
wins the blue ribbon in a thank-you note. That wouldn't be
sporting or courteous. How could I tell you which solution
I had chosen before I carried it out? You might not kill me,
but you would certainly try to queer my plans. I would almost
have to count on it. No, on occasion, you shall have to check
your newspapers and magazines (the better ones, mind you;
avoid the tabloids; this story will be too refined to pierce the
calloused sensibilities of such editors). Trust me, media manipulation is an old hobby of mine. Until that time, rest
comfortably knowing that our correspondence is safety copied on heavy bond of the best thread, and that in my spare
time I have reread these missives, and considering how noble

the epistolary exchange is as a literary tradition and how fine these letters read when taken as a single work, I have thought about submitting them to the editors of one of the finer houses. I realize there is risk in it, and yet, why not? The millennium approaches.